Let's set the ground rules
for our honeymoon

"Item one: you sleep on couch. Item two: public displays of affection." Mandy stared at him for a long, dispassionate moment, then lowered her head and began to write. "I don't care for public displays. The station wants film of a honeymoon couple, so I imagine they'll want us to hold hands and make sheep's eyes at each other, but that's it, understand?"

Reaching up to gingerly massage his neck, he nodded his agreement. "Item three: pet names," Josh said, pointing to her hand as if he wanted her to write down his words. "I will allow dear, darling and the occasional sweetheart. I will not allow honeybun, sweetcheeks or snookums. They're demeaning."

Mandy wrote down every word, then tapped the page firmly with the pencil tip. "Right. No sickening pet names. Message heard and understood—doll face."

"Fair enough, carrot top," Josh said without a blink. "See, I knew we could work out everything."

Dear Reader:

The spirit of the Silhouette Romance Homecoming Celebration lives on as each month we bring you six books by continuing stars!

And we have a galaxy of stars planned for 1988. In the coming months, we're publishing romances by many of your favorite authors such as Annette Broadrick, Sondra Stanford and Brittany Young. Beginning in January, Debbie Macomber has written a trilogy designed to cure any midwinter blues. And that's not all—during the summer, Diana Palmer presents her most engaging heros and heroines in a trilogy that will be sure to capture your heart.

Your response to these authors and other authors of Silhouette Romances has served as a touchstone for us, and we're pleased to bring you more books with Silhouette's distinctive medley of charm, wit and—above all—romance.

I hope you enjoy this book and the many stories to come. Come home to romance—for always!

Sincerely,

Tara Hughes
Senior Editor
Silhouette Books

KASEY MICHAELS

Compliments
of the Groom

Silhouette *Romance*

Published by Silhouette Books New York
America's Publisher of Contemporary Romance

To Jean Herman,
who knows just what it took to write this book.

SILHOUETTE BOOKS
300 E. 42nd St., New York, N.Y. 10017

Copyright © 1987 by Kathie Seidick

ISBN: 0-373-08542-7

First Silhouette Books printing November 1987

America's Publisher of Contemporary Romance

Printed in the U.S.A.

KASEY MICHAELS

considers herself a "late bloomer," having written her first romance novel after devoting seventeen years to her husband, four children, the little league and the avoidance of housework. She has published several Regency romances under both the name Kasey Michaels and Michelle Kasey, and has written, under her own name, Kathryn Seidick, a non-fiction book about her son's kidney transplant. *Compliments of the Groom* is Kasey's thirteenth book.

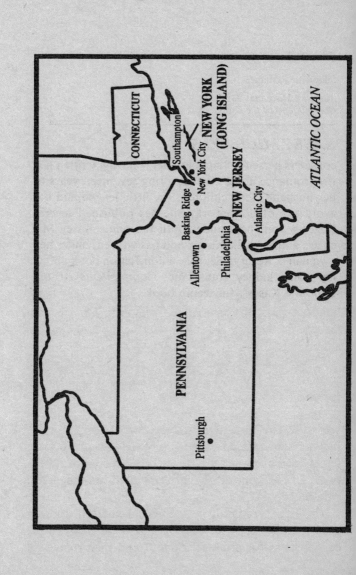

Chapter One

I won! I won! I won!"

Amanda Elizabeth Tremaine grabbed her friend's hands, pulling the astonished woman to her feet, and danced her around the room, alternately laughing and shouting.

"Mandy! Control yourself," Jeanne Tisdale pleaded, trying hard to catch her breath as she straightened her topknot, which had started to slip to one side as the younger woman's enthusiasm took its toll. "What did you win? The Irish sweepstakes? You're hopping about like some demented leprechaun! Wait! Let me sit down. I just got done wrestling with a whole room of terrible twos. I need your craziness like I need another homicidal toddler."

The grinning Mandy at last brought herself to order, gasped a sincere, "I'm sorry, Jeanne, I guess I got kinda carried away for a minute there," and then ruined her attempt at an apology by throwing her hands high over her head and whooping, "But *I won*!"

Jeanne Tisdale, head instructor of the Happy Days Nursery School for more years than she cared to count, was accustomed to the exuberance of her young assistant, and now simply sat back in her desk chair and waited for the whirlwind that was Mandy to blow herself out.

Jeanne didn't know what had set the young redhead off in the first place, except for the fact that it must have had something to do with the phone call Mandy had been pulled out of her prekindergarten class to answer. Donning her glasses and then pretending an interest she didn't feel in the budget report lying on her desk, Jeanne ignored Mandy's outburst, treating her colleague to a little child psychology.

It worked. Within moments Mandy was standing in front of her, palms flat on the desk. "Well? Aren't you happy? Aren't you wildly, deliriously happy? I mean it was a one-in-a-million—or at least several thousand—chance that I'd win, let alone walk away with first place. Why aren't you dancing with joy?"

"Amanda, my dear child," Jeanne said calmly, looking up into the younger woman's widely smiling face. "I'm forty-three years old. I just spent three hours with Justin Brosious, Todd Terrance Tillson, Sean 'Mad Dog' O'Connor and a dozen other damp-bottomed terrors. I couldn't dance with joy if Robert Redford waltzed in here and threw himself at my feet. Would you settle for a small *whoopee*—once I find out what I'm celebrating, that is?" she urged.

"Oh, I'm sorry," Mandy exclaimed penitently, running a hand through her short crop of burnished curls. "I guess I got a little carried away."

"Just a tad," Jeanne put in, grinning in spite of herself as Amanda pretended to look crestfallen at her employer's easy agreement with her admission of guilt.

At last, giving a huge, theatrical sigh, Mandy sat herself down in a straight-backed chair in front of the desk. "I guess you want me to start at the beginning, don't you?"

"It seems as good a place as any."

Mandy narrowed her emerald-green eyes and tried to look menacing, but it was clear that Jeanne didn't feel the least bit intimidated. "You're getting crotchety in your old age, Miss Tisdale, did you know that?" She shook her head back and forth sorrowfully, although the movement failed to hide the dimple that had appeared in her left cheek. "Maybe you need more fiber in your diet."

"Or maybe I just need to put one Miss Amanda Tremaine on permanent finger paint duty," Jeanne suggested, leaning back in her chair and looking at the young teacher from over her horn-rimmed reading glasses.

Holding up her hands in mock surrender, Amanda gave up the fight. "You remember how the stereo broke last month, and how we haven't been able to afford a replacement?" she began before Jeanne could think up some worse punishment.

Jeanne nodded, grimacing. The school's constant lack of funds was a constant thorn in her side.

"Well, the day after the old stereo kicked the bucket I happened to hear about a contest on WFML—you know, that hard-rock radio station they play in the coffee shop across the street—and, surprise, surprise, they were having a contest to give away records, T-shirts, and, oh, all sorts of prizes, with the top prize to be a state-of-the-art stereo system. It was fate, surely you can see that!"

Mandy began wiggling in her chair, once more looking like she was about to erupt. "And I won *first prize!*"

Jeanne was speechless. It was like the answer to a prayer. It would be months before the trustees got around to replacing the stereo. "But, Mandy, dear," she asked after she had taken a moment to think about it, "don't you want the prize for yourself? I mean, I think it's wonderful that you should want to donate the stereo to the school, but have you even stopped to consider—"

"It's huge, Jeanne," Mandy broke in, waving a hand in dismissal. "I'd have no place to put it. Besides, Mrs. Thorton would throw me out on my ear if I played the thing above a whisper. I'll just reserve the right to play some of my own albums on it after school hours."

Jeanne looked intently into Amanda's guileless face and realized she was being totally honest. After entering the contest with the school in mind, it would never occur to her to renege once she had won first prize. "What did you have to do to win?" she asked at last. "I hope it wasn't anything too silly. I've heard about those radio contests. Remember the billboard sitters a couple of years ago? If you're going to be featured as nut of the week in *People* magazine, love, I don't think the board of trustees is going to be too ecstatic."

Mandy giggled, thinking of the straitlaced board and their reaction if she had been in one of those contests that had contestants riding rocking horses for three days or diving into swimming pools filled with Jell-O to win a new car. "Oh, no," she assured her quickly. "I didn't have to do anything except complete a sentence. You know—one of those twenty-five words or less things."

Jeanne saw Mandy lower her dark lashes to hide eyes that couldn't conceal a lie, and a strange, nervous churning began in her stomach. "What was the sentence, Amanda?'' she prodded gently, not really wanting to hear the answer.

"Well," Mandy began, her voice so low Jeanne had to strain to hear her. "It was just one of those silly questions. You know—like...um...like, oh, I eat this cereal *because*, or I like this car best *because*, or...um...we make love best to music because—that sort of thing. What does it matter what the question was?'' she hurried on, her tongue nearly tripping over itself. "It was just a silly—''

"What!" the older woman shouted, abruptly sitting up straight in her chair and putting her reading glasses in grave danger of dropping off the end of her nose.

Mandy rushed into speech. "It was a contest for newlyweds. Just a silly stunt. I just made up some drivel and sent it in. I never really thought I'd win.'' She tilted her head and smiled reminiscently. "Though actually, it *was* rather good—all that malarkey about moonlight and bearskin rugs.''

"Oh, good grief. She's proud of herself yet! But you aren't even married, Mandy,'' Jeanne felt forced to point out, shaking her head in disbelief. "Or did you, I sincerely hope, use a made-up name?''

Now the innocent green eyes stared straight at her employer and friend. "Jeanne!'' Mandy admonished in the same tone she used to point out the error of their ways to naughty toddlers caught in some mischief. "That would be cheating. Of course I didn't use a fictitious name. How could I? Besides, then they wouldn't have been able to find me when I won,'' she pointed out rationally. "I just—er—I just sort of *smudged* my 'Ms.' so that it looked more like a 'Mrs.'''

"Oh, I see. Innocent dishonesty,'' Jeanne answered dully, pressing her fingertips to her suddenly throbbing temples. Mandy was a wonderful person, cheerful, a good teacher and a joy to be around—but, oh, she did have a way of seeing the most outrageous things in a seemingly plausible way.

"Oh, don't you go all stodgy on me," Mandy complained, making a great business out of smoothing down a wrinkle in her denim skirt. "I wrote the best entry. That's all there is to it. Tomorrow I go down to the station to pick up my prize, and that's the end of it. Besides, aren't you sick of trying to make that tired old portable phonograph play 'Ring Around a Rosie' without coming out sounding like a funeral dirge?" To prove her point, Mandy slipped down to one knee and started groaning slowly, "R-i-n-g-g-g a-r-r-o-u-n-d-d—" until Jeanne broke in with another argument against the scheme.

The two women went round and round for a few minutes, Jeanne trying to point out possible pitfalls and Mandy just being Mandy. In the end, Mandy—possibly aided by her soulful rendition of "Ring Around a Rosie"—won the battle. The stereo system was to be looked upon as a gift from a generous, unnamed benefactor, and that and the fact that they would not have to allocate the funds for a new system themselves, should be enough to satisfy the board of trustees.

"I have the day off tomorrow anyway," Mandy said once everything was settled. "All I have to do is show up, identify myself as 'Ms-rs' Amanda Tremaine, and pick up my prize. See? It's that simple."

The offices of WFML—both the radio and the television stations operated out of the same building—were situated atop a medium-sized hill just outside the city of Allentown. It was a modern building, Mandy saw as she pulled her aged compact car into the visitors' parking lot, but it didn't appear to be nearly as artistically flamboyant as she always thought a place of media magic should look.

She took a moment to inspect her light makeup in the rearview mirror, hoping she looked innocent enough to pull off her plan. She was going to make a clean breast of things, she had decided after an almost sleepless night spent examining her conscience and discovering she didn't have enough latent larceny in her soul to go through with a deception of this magnitude.

She'd explain her reason for the fib she had told on the entry form and then throw herself on the deejay's mercy. Surely he'd understand and give her the stereo anyway. After all, hers *was* the best entry.

Stepping from her car, she took a moment to straighten her "newlywed outfit"—Jeanne's navy-blue polyester blouse with its floppy bow, white polyester pleated skirt, low-heeled white pumps and white vinyl shoulder bag. Only her bright red hair, tossed this way and that by the warm summer breeze that swept up the hillside, marred her squeaky-clean image—an image she hoped would keep Vic Harrison, the deejay she was soon to meet, from making any lewd comments about her winning entry.

Mandy moistened her suddenly dry lips, took a deep, steadying breath and made for the entrance. The double glass doors opened onto a small, chrome-and-glass decorated reception area holding a burgundy vinyl couch, an empty umbrella stand, an imposing-looking teak desk and an equally imposing-looking female Mandy took to be either the receptionist or the resident bouncer.

"I—er—I'm here to see Mr. Vic Harrison," she began in a rush, hating the nervous tremble she could hear in her voice. "It's silly really, making all this fuss, I mean.

I mean—really—they could have just as easily *sent* the thing couldn't they? After all—"

"Your name," the receptionist barked in her baritone, drillmaster voice, effectively putting a halt to Amanda's rambling tongue.

"Ah, yes." Mandy grimaced, girding herself up to face the music. Oh, well, what better place to do it than a radio station. "My name?" She gave a little laugh, as if there was something quite amusing about her name. "Right. My name." She bent down over the desk to peer at the paper the receptionist was now holding in her hand. "I guess you have me listed there as Mrs. Tremaine, but, and I'm sure Mr. Harrison will think this is a *scream*, but it would seem—"

"Amanda Tremaine. Mrs. Amanda Tremaine," the receptionist cut in unemotionally, holding a red-tipped nail against a line of typing that was part of a long list of names. "Down the hall to your left, you'll see the freight elevator. The lobby elevator is being serviced. Second floor, three corridors down to your right, third doorway. Don't go in if the red light is on."

"Yes, but—" Mandy protested, but the receptionist had clearly dismissed her, picking up a phone and pushing an extension number. "Mrs. Tremaine is on her way up," she said without preamble. Replacing the phone on the receiver, she looked owlishly at the lingering Mandy, who hurriedly click-clacked off down the tiled corridor in her sensible, low-heeled white pumps.

"Attila the Hun could have learned from that dame," she mumbled under her breath, looking around her for the freight elevator. "I *hate* elevators; I've *always* hated elevators. I'm only going to the second floor; I could have walked. That's what's the matter with people today. They're lazy. I ought to go back to the Dragon Lady and demand to know where the heck the stairs are. And I should stop talking out loud to myself, before somebody comes and takes me away!''

The elevator door took its own sweet time in opening, revealing a second cagelike door that she had to push aside manually in order to enter. Mumbling and grumbling to herself, she kept her head bowed and pushed with all her might. Mandy then stepped just inside the huge elevator and pulled the door closed behind her. She reached over to push the button for the second floor before facing front to stare hard at the lighted number panel, not trusting the elevator one little bit.

The machine began its ascent with a jerk and Mandy watched encouragingly as the light went out behind the number one and held her breath, silently cheering for number two to light up and the door to open. But just as quickly as the light went on it blinked off, and the elevator gave another jerk, breathed a loud wheeze and then settled itself firmly between the two floors.

"Oh, Lord," Mandy exclaimed aloud. "God's getting me for lying!" Looking toward the ceiling she raised her hands and complained, "Didn't you get the message—I've already promised to go straight!"

The man leaning a shoulder lazily against the rear wall of the elevator had lifted his brows in silent approval of the feminine form that stood before him, then realized he had been so preoccupied with his own thoughts that he had somehow forgotten to get off at the first floor and that the elevator was moving again.

After inspecting the female all the way down to her slim, well-turned ankles, he allowed his assessing gaze to return to the top of her frame, to linger on the riot of curls that he was sure had earned her the nickname of Carrot Top in grade school.

But this is no grade-school miss, he told himself, a small one-sided smile forming on his tanned face. She's done a good job trying to disguise the fact, but that's one very nice package she's hidden beneath that goody-two-shoes costume, he thought, idly wondering if she was here for a job interview and hoping to look every inch the competent professional.

The sharp jerking of the elevator as it came to an abrupt halt brought the man back to reality and he heard the female cry out.

"There's nothing to be alarmed about," he began in his most bracing voice, only to be cut off by Mandy's high-pitched yelp.

"Where—where did *you* come from?" she asked, whirling around to notice the other occupant of the elevator for the first time.

"Originally?" the man queried, his deep blue eyes crinkling a bit around the corners as he smiled a wide, lopsided grin. "My folks hail from Basking Ridge—that's a small town in New Jersey, you probably never heard of it—but I've lived in New York and Pennsylvania ever since college. You?"

"That's not what I meant and you know it!" Mandy shot back, looking up into a face that was, although she stood well over five feet tall, still some distance above her. "I didn't mean where did you come from, I meant where did you *come from*?"

The man raised his eyebrows a fraction and shrugged his shoulders. "Oh, even further back than that? Well, first, or so they tell me, I was nothing more than a gleam in my father's eye. Then—"

"Stop that!" Why do I have to get all the weirdos? Mandy asked herself, running a hand through her hair, ruining whatever was left of the prim style she had fashioned earlier. "It's just that I didn't see you when I got on. Do you think we'll be stuck here long? I hate elevators."

Lord, but she was a looker, the man thought, enjoying his first clear sight of Mandy's piquant little face. I especially like the turned-up nose, he thought privately. And the freckles, yeah, they're just the right touch. She definitely ranks in the top five of the ten women I would most like to be stuck in an elevator with—maybe even number three.

The man pushed himself away from the wall and walked over to the control panel. Pointing to the small cabinet fitted into the front of the elevator, he said, "Excuse me while I see if I can reach out and touch someone."

Opening the cabinet door, he then pulled out the emergency phone, while Mandy made a face behind his back. Smug, self-satisfied chauvinist, she accused silently.

After saying hello several times, he placed the receiver back on its hook and turned to comment cheerily, "Nobody home. I hope you've had your lunch."

"I'm being punished," Mandy decided, distractedly looking around her and seeing nothing but her prison—four walls of pea-green chipped paint—and her fellow prisoner, a first-class nut case. She closed her eyes and gave a defeated sigh. "I should have known this was going to happen," she moaned, once more giving in to her worst failing, thinking out loud. "Now the elevator is going to fall and I'll be killed and the funeral director will think I like the clothes I'm wearing. God, *please* don't let them bury me in polyester."

"Are you hysterical or is that outburst supposed to be in aid of something extremely deep?" her companion asked, once more leaning his broad shoulder against the elevator wall, all thoughts of his luncheon meeting forgotten as he watched Amanda's antics with growing good humor.

Mandy ignored his teasing sarcasm. "Do you work here?" she asked, taking in his casual faded jeans and T-shirt. *Tight, sexy* jeans and *form-fitting* T-shirt, she amended, blushing a bit in spite of herself.

"Who, me?" he responded, pointing a finger at his own chest.

"No," Mandy exploded, beginning to feel more than a little put upon. "I meant that pink hippopotamus over there in the corner. Of course, you!"

The man reached a hand up to his neck and straightened an imaginary old-school tie. "I'm in management."

"Great! It figures." Mandy exclaimed, throwing up her hands in disgust. "That's just peachy-keen dandy. I never yet met a manager who could so much as open a pickle jar."

I knew there was a fire raging under the girl-scout duds, the man comforted himself, enjoying the sight of Mandy's rapidly rising and falling bosom as her breathing quickened in her agitation. "You weren't expecting me to climb out that trapdoor up there and do the hero bit, were you? A person could get hurt doing that kind of thing, you know."

"Why couldn't you have been a janitor?" she demanded, skewering him with her eyes.

"Actually," he responded impishly, "I wanted to be a cowboy, but Mother had her heart set on college, you see, so—"

Hugging her arms around herself, she suddenly whirled away from him to block out the sight of his laughing face, even if she couldn't block out his voice. Sighing deeply, she muttered fatalistically, "Oh, what difference does it make anyway. I'm being punished, that's what it is. It was only a *little* fib, hardly even worth stopping an entire elevator for, for goodness' sake. Jeanne was right, oh, yes indeedy, she certainly was. *When* will I ever learn to look before I leap?"

The man, who seemed utterly invulnerable to any hints he should go stand in his corner and mind his own business, walked around to place himself directly in front of her. "Here's where I either kiss you senseless or throw cold water in your face. Which do you prefer?"

"What?"

"You're hysterical, lady," he told her calmly. "Haven't you ever been to the movies? It's standard Hollywood practice. You have your choice of treatment. Either that or you stop babbling about God getting you and tell me what has you in such an uproar. Come on, it will help pass the time till the Mounties come."

Why not? Mandy decided, thinking to make a clean breast of things before the cable snapped and sent them both plummeting to the basement. After all, much as he doesn't look the part, I guess he is only an innocent bystander. As long as he seems to be going down with me, he might as well know why.

Mandy took another look at the tall, dark, terribly handsome man smiling down at her and tried to pretend he was kindly Father Mulligan, her old parish priest from her hometown. It didn't work. He still looked more like a muscular Pierce Brosnan—and what woman in her right mind could see *him* as a priest?

Ah well, she temporized, like they say—any port in a storm. Amanda allowed him to take her hand and help her sit down on the floor, heedless of the hazard to Jeanne's pristine white skirt, and waited until he joined her before launching into a garbled version of her descent into sin.

"Is that all?" the man asked incredulously once she was done. "God, lady, if you're going to hell for that, where do you suppose they put Al Capone?"

"Don't try to cheer me up," Amanda said, causing her companion to issue a sharp bark of laughter. She shook her head at him. "Besides, in case you haven't figured it out yet—when this elevator goes, *you* go with it."

"This elevator is going to the second floor," he assured her yet again, knowing that deep down inside she already believed him but was just indulging what seemed to be a love of melodrama. "Besides," he added in bracing tones, "in your case there were certain extenuating circumstances."

"Such as?" Mandy asked, eager for absolution.

"Such as you weren't doing it for yourself but for all the poor musically deprived little tots at the day-care school."

"*Nursery* school," Mandy corrected. "It's church run, you know."

"Whatever," he conceded, disengaging his fingers from Mandy's and wrapping his hands around his knees, unaware that he had left her hand feeling strangely empty. "Just go in to this Harrison guy and brazen it out. What difference does it make whether or not you bent the rules a bit? It's not like it's *his* stereo. And bat those gorgeous eyelashes at him a few times while you're at it.

You'll probably have the poor sap throwing in a free stack of records."

Mandy began to relax. "You really think so?" she asked, impulsively grabbing his muscular forearm.

The man looked pointedly at her hand on his arm and then looked at her. "Oh, yeah," he breathed softly. "I really think so."

She couldn't help it. She blushed and tore her gaze away from his melting blue eyes. "I guess you think I'm a first-class idiot," she babbled nervously. "You know, I didn't really think the elevator was going to fall. Not *really*. I have this sort of weird imagination, you understand. The kids all love it; they say I tell the best stories at story time."

And I'd bet the ranch they all have happily-ever-after endings, he thought with a small smile.

She looked up again and saw that he was still staring at her in that same disturbing way. "After all," she went on, averting her eyes once more and playing with the straps on her purse, "it wasn't like I was planning on robbing the crown jewels or something. Or trying to take something just because I wanted it for myself. I mean, it *is* for the chil—"

A firm hand grasped her chin and turned her toward him, their gazes meeting and locking as he whispered huskily, "Lady, did anyone ever tell you that you talk too much?" Then he leaned forward and joined his lips softly with hers.

It was just the faintest whisper of a kiss; he demanded little more from her than that she let him move his mouth lightly against hers, but Mandy thought she could feel the earth moving beneath her.

It wasn't until an amused male voice penetrated her distracted thoughts that she understood that the elevator had at last completed its journey to the second floor. "Well, *hello* there," the voice sang out mischievously. "I wondered where you had gotten to. Helen didn't say you were bringing the lucky hubby along, Mrs. Tremaine. No wonder he's grinning like that—that was some letter!"

"Uh—*what*?" Mandy stammered, looking up to see a man who could only be Vic Harrison opening the cage-like inner door. "This isn't what you—I mean, this man isn't—You thought?—Oh, no, you see—"

"This man had better be Mr. Tremaine, lady," the disc jockey interrupted as Mandy tried vainly to think up a suitable story—yet another lie would only compound her sin. "If he isn't, you must hold the record for fooling around in the shortest time after the knot's been tied!"

The man who had been sitting beside her on the elevator floor, his hands draped negligently across his pulled-up knees—the man who had so lately heard her confession and had even more recently taken advantage of her agitation by kissing her—now stood up and held out his hand to the leering Harrison.

"Mr. Harrison?" he said cordially in his deep, husky voice. "I'm Mr. Tremaine. You'll have to excuse the wife here. We haven't been married long, you know, and she still gets a little flustered whenever I kiss her. You understand how it is," he ended, winking at the disc jockey in a way that had Mandy aching to choke them both.

The disc jockey looked back and forth between the two of them, taking in Mandy's high color and her husband's complacent grin, and decided to shake hands and get the show on the road. He was due back on the air in fifteen minutes.

"Follow me, Mr. and Mrs. Tremaine," he said, starting off down the hallway. "I tried to get hold of you this morning to let you know about a change in our plans, but then I decided it would be more fun to tell you in person. It seems we have a little surprise for you two!''

Mandy shot her pseudo-husband a questioning look, but he merely shrugged his shoulders and took her hand. ''Just keep your mouth shut and smile, *Mrs*. Tremaine. I'll handle it from here on out. By the way,'' he whispered, leaning over so that his warm breath caressed her ear, ''what's your first name?''

''Mandy,'' she squeaked, feeling the tug of the quicksand that was rapidly pulling her down. ''Amanda Elizabeth Tremaine, actually.''

''Very nice, Amanda Elizabeth,'' he told her, giving her trembling hand a reassuring squeeze. ''And now, just for the record, what's *my* name?''

Mandy stopped dead in her tracks. What was his name? She hadn't used a man's name on her entry form. ''I don't know!'' she whispered brokenly, looking as if she were about to ruin everything by bursting into tears.

''No problem, Amanda Elizabeth,'' he returned suavely, not easing her trepidation by so much as a hair. ''Just call me Joe and we'll be fine. Just fine. Trust me.''

Mandy groaned and allowed herself to be led down the corridor to her fate.

''You're going on a *what!*''

Mandy pushed Jeanne back into her chair and cautioned her to remember she was an old lady of forty-three. ''I said, I'm going on a honeymoon.''

''I know that's what you said, Amanda,'' Jeanne snapped. ''I'm just trying to figure out *why* you said it. You can't go on a honeymoon, you idiot child. *You're not married!*''

''Oh, sure. And do you want me to tell Vic Harrison and all the people down at WFML that?'' Mandy asked sarcastically. "I had made up my mind to tell Mr. Harrison the truth when I got there and hoped he'd still give me the stereo, you know, but then Joe came along and suddenly things kind of got out of hand."

"Who's Joe?" Jeanne asked weakly.

"Joe says I could be charged with fraud, even if I didn't actually accept the prize, and unlawful receipt of goods before the fact or something like that, and—and I don't want to remember what else I could be charged with. Joe says—"

"Who's Joe?" Jeanne yelled, feeling like she had come in on the second reel of the movie.

"Joe Tremaine," Mandy explained, knowing how ridiculous her explanation must be sounding to the other woman.

Jeanne shook her head as if to clear it. "You don't *know* any Joe Tremaine. Mandy, you're not making any sense."

Mandy walked over to the state-of-the-art stereo that now held place of honor in the largest playroom of the Happy Days Nursery School and flicked away an imaginary fleck of dust. Then she took a deep, steadying breath and turned to face her worried employer.

"I got stuck in the elevator at the station," she said in a rush. "You know how I hate elevators. And there was this man in the elevator with me, and he asked me to tell him why I thought I'd be buried in polyester, and I told him about the stereo, and then he kissed me. And then Mr. Harrison saw us and thought he was my *husband*. So what does he go and do except introduce himself as Joe Tremaine, just like some knight in shining armor riding to the rescue."

"I think I'm getting a headache," Jeanne said in aid of nothing in particular.

"But then," Amanda went on as if she were in a hurry to get the telling done as quickly as possible, "Mr. Harrison goes and tells us about the honeymoon the station was giving us in Atlantic City for five days so they can film us for their nighttime-magazine television show. Well, we had already accepted the stereo, so you can see it was too late to do anything but grin and say, 'How perfectly wonderful, thank you very much.' Now Joe says if we ever tell the truth they'll arrest me, and maybe him, too, and so I have to go through with it—surely you can understand that—and that's why I'm going on a honeymoon."

She took another deep breath, spread her arms wide in resignation and said, "See, Jeanne, it's just like I said—simple!"

Jeanne Tisdale, not saying a solitary word, and looking neither right nor left, stood up and walked toward her classroom full of terrible twos. At the moment, they seemed to be the lesser of two evils.

Chapter Two

It was one thing to act bright and breezy in front of Jeanne, who had allowed herself to be convinced that nothing much could happen in Atlantic City with a cameraman, a technician and a female director along as constant chaperons, but it was quite another for Amanda to convince herself that five days spent with "Joe Tremaine" could be put down under the heading of harmless good fun.

Mandy had been due for a vacation, so it wasn't the time away from the school that bothered her. Nor did she feel overly concerned with the reaction of the trustees. As she had told Jeanne, the local television station was only one of the thirty-three channels area residents could get on their cable TVs, and it was no secret that hardly anyone ever watched Channel 76—except to tune in the *Leave It To Beaver* reruns.

The chances that any of the trustees would ever see Mandy on television, let alone connect her with the school, were slim to nonexistent. Besides, Vic Harrison had already told her that the story would be only one of two on the half-hour show. Taking away time for commercials, Mandy figured she would have ten minutes of airtime, give or take a couple of seconds. If she wore dark glasses and kept her hair under a hat or scarf whenever possible, her own family wouldn't recognize her.

And therein lay the rub. For Mandy, above all, did not want to be recognized. If there had been even the slightest chance that the program would be shown outside the Allentown area she would have confessed her duplicity on the spot, and damn the consequences. She had built a nice life for herself in the city over the past three years, and even a state-of-the-art stereo and a stern lecture for having tried to pull a fast one to win the contest were not enough to have her willingly jeopardize her hard-won freedom.

Lastly, there remained Joe Tremaine himself. When the deejay had sprung his "surprise" on the two of them, Mandy had been sure Joe would call a halt to the deception. After all, even if he were really the last true Samaritan left this side of the Mississippi, there remained limits to the good-neighbor policy. It was one thing for him to jump in and get Mandy over a rough patch at the station, but it was another to give up five whole days of his life to keep her secret safe.

Didn't he have a job he had to go to? He certainly didn't dress like a man whose position allowed him to take time off whenever he felt the urge.

Yet somehow Mandy didn't believe Joe Tremaine was just a "fellow American down on his luck" who would look on a stay in Atlantic City as a free meal ticket. His appearance offered too many contradictions. His hair was professionally styled, for one thing, and he may have been wearing sneakers, but they were top-of-the-line running shoes, not K-Mart specials. Then there was his watch—a slim gold wafer that Mandy recognized as being the same Swiss brand her ridiculously wealthy grandfather favored. No, money was not the answer.

So what was in it for him?

Climbing out of the huge, claw-footed tub that had been the main reason she had agreed to live in the third-floor walk-up in the first place, Mandy caught sight of herself in the full-length mirror that hung behind the door. She examined her reflection for a moment, considering.

"Naw," she scorned at last, remembering how truly good-looking Joe Tremaine was. "No matter what his problem is, he's not that hard up."

The man Mandy still knew only as Joe Tremaine walked briskly down the tiled corridor and pushed open the door that led into the executive offices of WFML. It was after hours and the secretary who sat behind the desk guarding the owner's private sanctum was gone for the day.

Without stopping to knock on the double wooden doors, he entered the executive office and headed straight for the tiled shower that was part of the suite, dropping his sneakers, jeans and T-shirt haphazardly along the way.

He wasn't usually sloppy but tonight he was in a hurry. He had a date with his "wife."

A scant fifteen minutes later he was once again in the executive office, now dressed in white duck slacks and a faded sea-green collarless Panama Jack shirt that he knew looked good with his tan. Slipping his bare feet into a pair of loafers he had found stuffed under the desk, he was just putting his billfold in his front pocket when the door from the secretary's office opened.

"Going out on the town, Josh?" the older man asked, lowering himself gingerly into a chair. "I should have known it wouldn't take you more than a day in town to get yourself lined up with one of the local beauties. Who is she, that cute little thing in Production? Lord, it's been a long day. I'm bushed. I just thought I'd stop by to hear your first impressions before heading back to the hotel. So? Do you think we made a good deal? I've always wanted to own my own television station. The radio end of it was just a bonus."

The whole time the older man had been talking, the man he had called Josh was busy, combing his hair in front of the mirror that hung over the credenza on the far wall, tucking his shirt into his slacks, buckling a belt around his lean waist, and lastly, checking through a manila file folder that lay on the desktop and then scribbling down the address he had been looking for on a sheet torn from the desk calendar.

"I like the station fine, Dad," he said now, walking around the desk to sit down in a chair that faced his father's. "In fact, I think I like your 'bonus' best of all."

"Don't tell me you've always had some latent yearning to be a disc jockey, Josh. Wasn't it enough your poor mother and I had to live through a decade of those skipping rocks you always had blasting away in your room?"

"Skipping rocks?" Josh looked puzzled for a moment, then grinned. "Those were the Rolling Stones, Dad, and I still buy all their albums. But no, I don't want to be a disc jockey. As a matter of fact, I find I have to be out of town for the next several days. Do you think you can handle the paperwork on this project yourself?"

The older man, who looked much like his son except for the gray hair at his temples and the slight bulge around his waistline, stood up, taking exception to Josh's last words. "I've been handling things since before you cut your milk teeth, you impertinent pup! I only asked you along on this trip because a radio-television station sounded like fun. This whole investment is small potatoes and you know it. I just thought I needed a hobby, that's all."

Josh looked around the expensively decorated office. "Some hobby. It's a good trick you didn't decide to dabble in railroads. I don't think even Phillips, Inc. is up to turning a profit from Amtrak. But seriously, Dad, with a little work this place could be holding its own in a couple of years. You could start by scaring up a weather girl for the six o'clock news."

"Now we're talking about *your* hobby, Joshua. Women! So who's the lucky female tonight? You didn't tell me."

Joshua Phillips rose from his chair and walked toward the door, picking up his silk sports jacket as he went and slinging it over his shoulder. Slanting his father the one-sided smile that had boded no good ever since his toddler days, he said, "No, I didn't, did I? Put a candle in the window, Dad, I may be late."

Mandy was just adjusting the window fan so that it would blow more fully on her as she lay on the sofa watching the evening news when she heard a loud knock at her door. Her first thought was that it was the repairman, actually showing up as promised to fix her broken air conditioner, and she nearly flew to the door to open it, saying, "Thank God you finally got here! I'm burning up!"

Josh Phillips was leaning against the doorjamb, his jacket hooked over his shoulder, feeling slightly winded after climbing three airless flights of stairs in the late-afternoon heat. His blue eyes twinkled appreciatively as he took in the sight of Mandy as she stood holding the door wide open, wearing cut-off denims, a sleeveless blouse tied up under her midriff and little else.

"I always wanted to be a fireman, too," he said, easing himself away from the doorjamb and ducking under Mandy's arm to enter the apartment. "Next thing you know you'll want to play doctor, and then all my fantasies will be complete."

Mandy slammed the door and whirled to confront the intruder, who stood in the middle of her suddenly small living room grinning like the Cheshire cat. "Are you naturally crude, or do you work at it?" she asked, hands on her hips and feeling more than a little abused. "I thought you were the repairman. My air conditioner is on the fritz."

"I don't know who Fritz is or why he's holding up your air conditioner, but I'd say he's a lucky man to still be alive. You know, if looks could kill, I'd be a dead man, and all I did was knock on your door." Without waiting for an invitation, Josh surveyed the room and then walked over to inspect the ailing appliance. "What's wrong with it?"

Mandy threw up her hands and gave up the fight. Clearly there was no way she was going to get through to this man that she wasn't in the mood for company. "It doesn't make good toast anymore," she said, throwing herself back down on the couch and trying hard to pretend she didn't feel like she was soon to expire from heat prostration. The top floor of a three-story building was no place to be in the middle of a heat wave. The bath she had taken when she first got home had long since lost its cooling effect.

"Feeling just the tiniest bit bitchy this evening, are we?" Josh asked, taking in Mandy's frowning face and thrust-out lower lip. "Get me a screwdriver like a good girl, won't you?"

"A screwdriver?" she repeated anxiously. "Why?"

Josh cast her a look that boded no good for her if she refused. "A *Phillips* screwdriver," he clarified, giving her a strange grin.

Rolling her eyes, she threw her legs to one side and stood up, looking for all the world like a martyr about to be thrown to the lions. "I think you're beating a dead horse. Besides," she added nastily as she grudgingly went to do his bidding, "you said you're in management. The only screwdriver you'd probably know how to use worth a darn is made with vodka and orange juice."

"And get dressed, we're going out," he said as she slapped the screwdriver into his palm as if he were a surgeon who'd just called for a scalpel. "Not that you don't look fetching, wife, but I'm in no mood to beat away every man we meet with a stick. Married women shouldn't look like they're still advertising." Turning his head, he set about unscrewing the front panel of the air conditioner.

Mandy opened and closed her mouth several times until she realized she must look like a fish gasping for air and then looked down at her blouse and shorts. She wasn't "advertising," she was just trying to stay cool. And in the privacy of her own home, too! Who did he think he was, anyway?

She opened her mouth one more time to tell the man where he could put his comments—and maybe even his screwdriver—when the low hum of the air conditioner caught her attention. "There we go," Josh was saying, wiping his hands together in satisfaction. "Just a loose wire. You should clean your filter once in a while, you know. This thing's disgusting."

Mandy's hands bunched into fists. Just as she had been about to thank him for fixing the air conditioner he had insulted her housekeeping. Why, for two cents she'd—

"You still here?" he asked, the front panel of the air conditioner now back in place. "Come on, chop, chop. I've got reservations at seven at the Hilton."

"I don't care if you've got reservations at nine on the moon!" Mandy declared, at last finding her voice. "I'm not going anywhere with you."

Josh shook his head sadly, his smile full of pity. "Yes, you are, wife. Or did you forget that we leave on our honeymoon this Saturday? I thought we'd better put our heads together to make sure we keep our stories straight all next week."

"Oh," she said in a small voice. "That."

Now his smile was full of something else, something that did strange things to her insides. "Yes, *that*. I guess we could just as easily stay here and call out for pizza," he offered, deliberately raking her with his eyes while twirling an imaginary mustache. "I'm flexible."

Mandy was already on her way out of the room.

"You don't live around here?" Mandy asked, noticing that Josh had referred to a folded map he had picked up from the front seat of his car before moving off down Fifteenth Street for Hamilton Mall. Looking around the interior of the sedan, she went on in a rush: "This is a rental car, isn't it? You could be a serial killer, couldn't you? What am I doing getting into a car with you? Stop at the corner, I want to get out."

Josh sent her a quick look as he merged into the traffic. "A serial killer? Do I look like a serial killer?"

Mandy looked him up and down through narrowed eyelids. He looked like he should be doing ads for some expensive brand of Scotch. He looked expensive. He looked sexy. He looked—"How should I know how a serial killer looks?" she protested rationally, blushing a bit at the line her thoughts were taking. "If people could tell how they looked they wouldn't get into cars with them and end up dead on back country roads, would they? Didn't you hear me, let me out of here!"

To show her seriousness, she began pulling on the door handle, but the car was one of those child-proof models and she couldn't unlock it from her side. Giving up, she gave the door a last whack with her hand and muttered, "So much for safety-conscious Detroit. Now what do I do?"

Josh had been watching her as she struggled with the door, looking like a child frustrated by the lid on a cookie jar, and shook his head. "Will you quit it, Amanda Elizabeth? I'm no serial killer. Now sit still like a good girl and tell me where to turn."

Mandy kept her head down but raised her eyes to look through the windshield to see where they were. "Left at the corner," she said grudgingly. "And don't call me 'girl.' It's chauvinistic."

Josh pulled the car into the parking lot and guided it into the space the attendant indicated. Turning off the engine, he unlocked the doors from his side and said, "There you go, *woman*, you're free to roar now. Go ahead, make a run for it. But, please, don't ask me to hold the door for you. I wouldn't want you to think I don't believe in equal rights."

"That's not equal rights, that's common courtesy," Mandy pointed out, then sat back in the seat and crossed her arms. "Equal rights doesn't mean men have to regress to a caveman mentality."

Snapping his fingers as if in disappointment, Josh said, "And here I was looking forward to dragging you off to my lair by the scalp. Pity. I guess I'll have to settle for dinner, that is if you've decided I'm not some deranged killer who's offering dinner and a murder."

Mandy waited until Josh had walked around and helped her out of the car before replying. "I'm sorry about that. I guess I've seen too many hysterics on Donahue. But you know I'm right. I really don't know anything about you."

Slipping his arm around her waist, Josh led her to the sidewalk. "So you have nothing else to do but trust your own judgment, right? I guess I could get you a note from my mother, but then who's going to vouch for her?"

Mandy bristled. "I've said I'm sorry, Joe. You don't have to beat me over the head with it. Here's the entrance. Come on, I'm hungry."

Without waiting for his agreement, Mandy pushed open the door and started inside. Josh hung back a moment, admiring the way her simple yellow sundress showed off her shapely legs and slim ankles, then said under his breath, "Josh Phillips, you have just entered the Twilight Zone. Relax and go with the flow."

Within minutes they were seated in a cozy wraparound corner booth, their menus spread in front of them. "We'll go Dutch, naturally," Mandy said, looking at the prices.

"Why naturally? I invited you."

"Because this dinner is strictly business," Mandy answered reasonably, mentally choosing the fried chicken although she was positively drooling for a thick, juicy steak. "You're right, we have to discuss this stupid fool stunt you talked us into."

"I talked us into—*I talked us into*—well, I like that!" Josh exclaimed, causing a few heads to turn in their direction. "Lady, you ought to consider leaving your brain to science!"

Mandy peeked over the top of her menu and saw that they were becoming the center of attention. Burying her face behind the menu, she warned in a whisper, "*Shh!* You're making a scene." Then she turned her head to look at him accusingly. "And it is too your fault. I was only at the station to make a clean breast of things. I never intended to defraud or default or whatever it is you said I was going to do. *You're* the one who jumped in with both feet, smiling that sickening smile and saying, 'Hi, I'm Mr. Tremaine' and then *winking* in that horrid way like you and Vic Harrison had some dirty secret between you."

"That's another thing," Josh cut in swiftly. "What did you say in that twenty-five words or less of purple prose you sent in that had Harrison leering at you like you were his first cupcake after a long diet of celery? I've only known you a few hours and already your imagination scares me to death."

"Don't change the subject!" Mandy gritted her teeth and buried her head once more in the menu.

Josh's eyebrows rose a fraction. "That good, eh? Remind me to ask the director about it when we meet Saturday morning."

Mandy closed her eyes and tried to concentrate on the memory of the delighted children who had danced and sung all that afternoon to the tunes that filled the playroom courtesy of the new stereo. It was worth it, she told herself over and over in a soundless chant. It was all worth it.

"It's not worth it," she said aloud, turning on the banquette to look at Joe, all her fears and frustrations in her eyes.

"Oh, come on," he assured her, still thinking she was talking about her entry, "it couldn't have been that bad. I mean, I'm not looking for Michener. Don't underrate yourself, Mandy. It was good enough to win, wasn't it?"

She shook her head back and forth rapidly in frustration. "Would you take your mind out of the gutter for a moment and listen to me? I don't mean the entry wasn't worth it. I mean that the whole thing isn't worth it." She laid the menu down with a decisive snap. "I can't go through with it. I'm sorry."

Josh took one look at Mandy's tear-bright eyes and waved away the waiter who had approached to take their drink order. What had begun the day before as a lark of the moment had, just this past afternoon, become a deadly serious project on Josh's part. No way was he letting Amanda back out now.

Putting down his menu, he reached over and took her hands in his. "Amanda, I—I need your help," he improvised wildly. "Amanda, look at me. I realize I'm going to have to level with you."

She tilted her head and looked at him, surprised at the seeming seriousness in his tone. "You need *my* help? How? Why? What are you talking about?"

Josh rubbed his forehead a moment, then looked around the dining room as if to check to make sure that no one was within earshot. "There are *things*—faintly shady things—that can go on in radio and television stations. Things that groups such as the FCC investigate."

Mandy bit her lip and looked around, not knowing what she should be searching for but careful nonetheless. "You're a government agent?" she asked in a breathy whisper, already caught up in the thrill of the thing. "Something's not as it should be at WF—I mean, at *you know where*—is it?"

"Now, Amanda," he warned solemnly, "don't get carried away. I never *said* I was a government agent, did I?"

She leaned back in her seat, giving him a superior smile. "You can't throw me off that easily, *Joe Tremaine*. I wasn't born yesterday, you know. I thought that Vic Harrison guy had shifty eyes when we met him. What is it—bribes, payola, kickbacks?"

My, what a great big imagination you have, grandma, Josh thought, barely keeping a straight face. He never said he was an agent, he just said there could be problems with stations, although he had to admit to himself that he was walking a very thin line between subtle truth and downright lie. If he didn't have a very sound reason for going on with this deception he'd have kicked himself for being a cad of the highest order.

But he did have a reason, a very good reason, even if the thought of spending five days in Atlantic City with Amanda Elizabeth Tremaine could only be looked upon as the best fringe benefit since the dental plan.

His voice lowered to a husky whisper, he leaned forward confidentially. "All of the above, Mandy, all of the above."

No matter how hard Mandy pushed, and she pushed with all of her considerable might, Josh refused to say anything else, reminding her that secret government assignments were always on a "need-to-know" basis. In fact, after mumbling that first reference to the FCC, he even refused to speak in initials.

But Mandy could live with that. What she couldn't live with was not knowing his real name. Joe Tremaine he was and Joe Tremaine he was going to stay. "You'll be less liable to slip up if you just keep thinking of me as Joe," he told her over dessert. It had been a memorable meal, served up between the small battles they had indulged in on every point, from his name to his supposed mission to the part the fake honeymoon would play in the "scenario."

In the end Josh had told her that the small station's only mobile cameraman, the one sure to be sent on this assignment, could be the subject of some investigation. It was a stroke of inspiration that finally satisfied Mandy and had Josh silently pitying the poor cameraman, who was sure to be confused by Mandy's interest in his every movement.

"Oh, I can hardly find room for this pie," Mandy said now, leaning back against the seat and putting a hand to her stomach. "That steak was so good I ate every last scrap. I'm glad you talked me into it."

"I have a generous expense account," Josh told her again. "We might as well make use of it. Even if I still can't see how you ate that meat. Every time you put your fork in it I thought it was going to moo."

"It's called Pittsburgh-rare," Mandy informed him, licking a last bit of whipped cream off the tip of her fork. "Burnt on the outside, nearly raw on the inside. The chef did it perfectly. Grandfather always said I was a cannibal, but to me it's the only way to eat good steak."

"Grandfather?" Josh repeated casually. "Does he live in town?"

Instantly Mandy was on the defensive. "Why do you want to know? You're investigating WFML, not me."

Easy, Phillips, easy, he cautioned himself. Flicking Mandy's cheek playfully, he said, "I just wanted to know if I was going to end up looking down the business end of a shotgun before this honeymoon is over. After all, grandfathers tend to be very protective of their unmarried granddaughters."

Her shoulders visibly relaxing, Mandy forced a smile. "You're right, I'm sorry I overreacted. No, Grandfather doesn't live around here. But if he did, you wouldn't be the only one in trouble. Not that he would be angry that I accepted the stereo under false pretenses, mind you. Oh, no, quite the contrary. It's helping you to uncover something illegal going on at the station that would get his blood boiling."

"He'd worry that you could get hurt?" Josh pushed, helping her out from behind the table after paying the check. "I can understand that, but I promise you, you'll be in no danger."

Mandy laughed shortly, shaking her head in the negative. "You've got the wrong end of the stick, Joe. When it comes to business dealings, well, let's just say Grandfather believes in the old adage 'all's fair in love and war.'"

"A real wheeler-dealer, huh?" They were outside the restaurant now, heading back to the garage to pick up the car.

"I think it's going to rain," Mandy commented, looking up at the darkening sky. "Maybe it will cool things off a bit."

It's getting cooler already, Josh thought as he helped Mandy into the front seat. Clearly the subject of Grandfather is off-limits. Your hunch of this afternoon is paying off so far, my boy, he congratulated himself silently, and two and two are still making four. Mandy *has* to be Alexander Tremaine's missing granddaughter. Revenge isn't a pretty word—and using an innocent like Mandy in your plan may not be all that noble—but old man Tremaine has it coming for what he did to Dave. Josh's handsome features hardened momentarily as he thought of his old college friend and how Alexander Tremaine's ruthlessness had destroyed first Dave's business, and then the man himself.

Josh allowed the companionable silence to continue while he drove the car around the block and headed west. He turned the radio on and tuned in an easy-listening station, not wanting to break the mood as they rode out of town and into the suburbs.

"Where are we going?" Mandy asked at last, suddenly coming out of her reverie to realize they had just passed the brightly lit outdoor wave pool at Dorney Park. "I thought you were taking me home."

Mandy could barely make out Josh's profile in the dim light of early evening. "You don't want to go back to that hot apartment yet, do you? Give the air conditioner some time to cool things off. Besides, I want to see a bit of your fair city while I'm here. What's that over there?"

"That's Wild Water Kingdom, the new water playground they built at the amusement park. It's got all sorts of water slides and a real wave pool. They've even had surfing contests in it. We took the nursery-school kids there already, and I think I had even more fun than they did. And got a sunburn that tormented me for a week!" she added, touching her shoulders gingerly in remembrance.

Josh turned his head to look at her. "Tender skin, Carrot Top?"

"Don't call me that!" she warned, jabbing his shoulder with her hand. "I've killed for less."

Pulling into the parking lot in front of a candle shop that was closed for the night, Josh stopped the car and turned off the ignition. "And hot-tempered too," he teased, knowing he was pushing his luck but loving every minute of it. "Don't you ever worry that you might be considered a stereotype?"

"Don't you ever worry that you might one day use that smart mouth of yours to bite off more than you can chew?" she shot back, wondering how she could have ever thought she could tolerate this man for nearly a week, no matter how noble her intentions.

Leaning back against the car door, Josh gave a low whistle. "Oh, heavens, I do believe I've just struck a nerve. I didn't mean to be insulting, you know."

"No, of course not," she agreed heatedly. "It just comes to you naturally doesn't it?"

"Hey, I like red hair. I even like freckles." Easing himself across the bench seat to sit next to her, he slid an arm around her shoulders. "I could even learn to like green eyes, given half a chance."

Mandy kept looking out the passenger-door window, refusing to turn her head even though she could feel the heat radiating from his body, he was sitting so close beside her. "Everybody likes green eyes," she said, closing hers so that she would not have to look into his beautiful blue ones. "And I am not a stereotype. I'm me. *You're* the stereotype."

That took Josh back a pace, just as he was reaching to run his fingers lightly up the side of Mandy's white throat. "Me? A stereotype?" he questioned. "How do you figure?"

Shifting in her seat to look at him, she explained, "Look at you. Collarless shirt, baggy white pants, no socks. Didn't I just see you in the latest issue of *TV Guide*?" She saw him wince, and knew she had scored a few points of her own. This little victory gave her courage, and she decided to go for the jugular. After all, all things considered, she'd had a very trying day, a very trying couple of days. "And then there's your hair," she pushed recklessly.

"What about my hair?" Josh asked tightly, his toes curling uncomfortably in his loafers.

"It's perfect, that's what. Your teeth are perfect. Your tan is perfect. Everything about you is perfect." She threw up her hands as if the enormity of his perfection was just too much to be borne. "You're just too darn perfect to be real, that's what. Why, if you weren't such a certifiable nut case I'd think you probably drive a Volvo!" She was really getting the bit between her teeth now. "And another thing—"

"There's one thing about me that's not perfect," Josh interrupted, not really ready to hear any more. "I'm not a perfect gentleman." So saying, he positioned his hand firmly on the back of Mandy's neck and as he lips met hers, he effectively cut off her cataloguing of his sins.

Chapter Three

Ouch! Where did you learn that nasty little trick, from one of your Dennis the Menace toddlers?" Josh sat back, gingerly touching the back of his neck just at the hairline. "That hurt."

"It was meant to," Mandy informed him, daintily arranging her skirt over her knees. "Now I suggest you start this car and head back to town before I really get nasty." She didn't try to hide her smile as she enjoyed her small triumph. Bless cable television for all its marvelous public-service programs, she thought, remembering where she had picked up that particular bit of self-defense. "You know, I've been thinking, Joe—it's time we talked about some ground rules for this honeymoon of ours."

Josh pulled back out onto the highway, still muttering under his breath. "How much hair did you take, anyway? I feel like I should be bleeding."

Mandy held up her right hand, wiggling her fingers at him. "Isn't it amazing that these delicate female hands can cause such havoc by merely tugging on those little hairs on the back of your head? It's all in the wrist, you know," she added smugly. Then, belatedly feeling sorry for him, she asked, "Is it really still bothering you? I never tried it before so I didn't know how hard to tug."

"Let's just say those delicate female hands of yours should be registered as lethal weapons, like a prize-fighter's fists." He finally stopped holding onto his neck, which really did hurt. "As for ground rules between the two of us, I begin to see the need for them myself. Either that, or I start packing a gun."

"Oh, don't do that. It would make such a nasty bulge under your pretty jacket," she quipped, still not ready to call a halt to their earlier discussion.

"Do these ground rules you want apply to personal swipes at each other? If not, I think I'd like to warble a few choruses about *your* choice of wardrobe."

Instantly bristling, she blurted out sarcastically, "Like what? What's the matter with my clothing? Not trendy enough for you? Perhaps you'd prefer something in low-cut gold lamé?"

Josh shot her a sidelong look, as if considering her proposal. "How low cut?"

"Never you mind! Now tell me what's wrong with my clothes!"

"You dress like a teenager, if that dress is representative of your wardrobe," he told her flatly. "I'm surprised you don't wear saddle shoes and knee socks."

Mandy looked down at her sundress as if seeing it for the first time. It was more than three years old, a leftover from her college days, as were most of her clothes. She hadn't bought much of anything since then except necessities. There had been no reason to, not to mention the money she would need to replace her wardrobe.

Maybe they did look more youthful than her twenty-four years warranted.

"Well? No snappy comeback? No counterattack, telling me I look like some fashion-magazine retread? Come on, Mandy, I asked for it. Sock it to me."

She pushed her chin down onto her chest. "Oh, shut up, will you? You've made your point. I apologize for attacking you, okay? Let's call a truce." There was no way she was going to admit to any lapses in her wardrobe, any more than she would tell him that, in her opinion, he looked better than any male-model fashion layout she'd ever seen.

"Sorry, but no. *Not* okay. You're supposed to be a happy newlywed. If the rest of your clothes look as virginal as that sundress, someone is going to smell a rat. I'll bet you even sleep in some long shirt with a picture of Snoopy on the front. I think we have to go shopping before we leave for Atlantic City."

Mandy wriggled uncomfortably in her seat, hating him for being right. "Ziggy," she muttered after a short silence.

"Huh?"

"My nightshirt has Ziggy on the front. You know, that short, fat, bald cartoon guy with the big nose. He's wearing a nightcap," she added for clarity. Her little confession over, she regained some of her spunk. "But if you think you're going to have anything to do with picking out my nightgowns you're out of your devious little mind! I'd as soon ask the Marquis de Sade to go shopping with me."

Josh conceded her this little victory. "All right, Mandy. Just as long as you remember that I'm not into leather or rubber. I do like black, though I guess that isn't very honeymoonish, is it?"

"I don't care if you like purple satin with pink stripes! You're not going to see any of my nightgowns anyway. Turn left up here."

Obeying her instructions, Josh realized that he had opened a can of worms he might have been smarter to leave shut. Clearly Mandy had not as yet thought about their sleeping arrangements. Just as clearly, he saw as he looked over to see her clutching the passenger-side door, her eyes wide with shock, she had thought of them now.

"About those ground rules—"

"Yes, wife?" he asked, grinning at her.

Her eyes narrowed as she glared at him in the dark car. "You're enjoying this, aren't you? First you land me in this mess, then when I try to call a halt to the deception you tell me some cock-and-bull story about how you need my help to investigate some shady dealings at the station—"

"I never said I was an investigator!" he interrupted, putting on the turn signal before making a right at the corner.

She glared at him for a moment before continuing. "I know I'm the gullible type, Jeanne tells me that all the time, but suddenly I have the feeling it's snowing in here and you're the snowman. Why, you won't even tell me your name." She sat up very straight. "I demand to see some identification! And pull over, we're home."

All the way up three long flights of stairs, Josh Phillips searched around wildly in his mind for a reason not to show her his driver's license, the form of identification she had demanded as he'd helped her out of the car. He couldn't be sure she would recognize his name—after all, the story of his company's takeover of WFML hadn't hit the papers yet—but his address was sure to ring a few warning bells in her head.

He stood quietly until she had fitted her key in the apartment door, opened it and stepped inside, flipping on the lights. The cool air in the living room was welcome after the long, hot climb and she momentarily abandoned him to go stand in front of the air conditioner, lifting her hair to let the cool air fan the back of her neck. Her eyes closed as she enjoyed the refreshing feeling and he quickly took that moment to remove his license from his billfold and stick it in his back pocket.

"Would a charge card suffice, Inspector?" he asked reasonably, holding out several he had pulled from the billfold. "I must have left my license in my other slacks after showing it at the car-rental place."

"'Phillips, Inc.,'" she read, wrinkling her nose as she flipped through the cards one by one. "These don't tell me anything. All of them are company cards. What is it, some dummy corporation like the CIA uses? Don't you have something with your name on it? Something with your blood type on it? I'll even settle for your library card. What would you do if you were in an accident? Nobody would know who you were."

"I know," he answered, settling himself comfortably on the couch. "I guess I've subconsciously fought against carrying around a lot of identification after all those years of having my name sewn into my underwear for summer camp. Besides, I still think it's a good idea if you keep on calling me Joe. I'll have enough on my mind as it is without worrying about you making some silly slipup and—um—giving the game away."

"Thank you for that rousing vote of confidence. I'm surprised you even thought to include me in your plans at all, if that's what you think." With a toss of her head,

Mandy disappeared into the small kitchen, to reappear carrying two tall glasses of iced tea. "Careful," she warned as she handed one to him, "it might be poisoned."

Josh took a long drink, then set the glass down on the coffee table and leaned back, his hands behind his head. "Ah, this is the life. Dinner out, a leisurely drive, and then home again for a cozy evening with the little woman. There, do I sound married enough to convince the television crew?"

Mandy looked longingly at the couch, the most comfortable piece of furniture in the whole apartment except for the bed, which was definitely out of bounds, and then opted to sit in the overstuffed chair she had picked up at a secondhand store.

Looking over at Josh, who was now flipping through the television guide and muttering something about seeing if there was a good ball game on, she could feel her anger building up inside her, ready to explode.

How had she ever gotten into this horrible situation? One minute she had been on top of the world, the winner of a brand-new stereo, and the next she had been forced into a deception that had been growing like Topsy ever since. How could she have agreed to this honeymoon trip? Was she out of her tiny mind?

Look at him, she told herself, making himself at home in my living room. If he tells me he's always wanted to play house, I'll bean him with the lamp! Aloud, she said, "All right, Joe, fun time's over. The stereo is already in the nursery-school playroom, and I'm committed to going through with the rest of this scheme. Wait, let me phrase that another way. I mean, the stereo is in the playroom and I should *be* committed!"

Josh lifted his gaze from the program listings and looked at Mandy as she sat in the big floral-printed chair, her legs tucked up under her skirt. "I really did think I was being helpful. You do know that, Mandy, don't you?"

He looked so sincere sitting there, his blue eyes staring unwaveringly into hers. Reluctantly, she allowed herself to be mollified. "Your heart was in the right place, I guess." As he grinned and made a move toward her she added dampeningly, "It's just a shame you had to end up with your foot in my mouth."

His smile faded slightly, but then he brightened. "Not really, Mandy. My original plan—trying to make people think I was an executive of some sort—isn't half as good as what I fell into with this honeymoon thing." Lord, he thought, lowering his eyes, it's amazing how a person can use the truth if he puts his mind to it.

"An executive?" Mandy snorted. "Not to belabor the point, Joe, but you look less like a hardworking executive than Donald Duck. Besides, you have a bigger problem. What if the cameraman you're zeroing in on isn't the one who's assigned to cover our honeymoon? What do you do then, James Bond, go back ten and punt?"

"I already told you he'll be the one," he assured her, silently wishing he could figure out some way to change the subject. He wouldn't be quite so intrigued with Mandy if she were dumb enough to fall for his ploy without a single murmur of doubt, but he hadn't prepared well enough for his ingenuity to hold up under this third degree. "I can't think of a better place than Atlantic City to get to know the guy a bit, watch his habits. He's bound to give himself away sooner or later, considering the information I've already picked up about his personal habits.''

"He gambles?" Mandy felt she was making the obvious conclusion.

Josh shook his head in the negative. "He drinks like a fish," he improvised, not wanting to spend the entire week watching Mandy chase the supposedly guilty cameraman through the casino, counting every quarter he dropped into the slot machines. "And he likes the ladies, so be careful not to pay too much attention to him. After all, I can't be with you all the time."

That statement brought back all of Mandy's earlier fears, banishing the cameraman and any thoughts she may have had of playing detective. "That's another thing, one of the first ground rules," she began, rising to seek out a pencil and paper to make a list. "Item one: our sleeping arrangements."

Josh sat back and folded his hands across his chest. "Before you go on, Miss Tremaine," he interrupted primly, "let me tell you—I'm not that kind of guy. I fully intend to sleep on the couch, so don't you go getting any weird ideas."

Mandy stared at him for a long, dispassionate moment, then lowered her head and began to write. "Right. Item one: Joe sleeps on couch. Item two: public displays of affection." She looked up at him, her small face assuming serious lines. "I don't care for public pawing. The station wants film of a honeymoon couple, so I imagine they'll want us to hold hands and look sheep's eyes at each other, but that's it, understand? Remember, I have more than that hair-tugging move in my bag of tricks."

Reaching up to gingerly massage his neck, Josh nodded his agreement. "Item three: pet names," he said, pointing to her hand as if he wanted her to write down his words. "I will allow 'dear,' 'darling' and the occasional 'sweetheart.' I will not allow 'honeybun,' 'sweet cheeks,' or 'snookums.' They're demeaning."

Mandy wrote down every word, then tapped the page firmly with the pencil tip. "Right. No sickening pet names. Message heard and understood—Doll Face."

"Fair enough, Carrot Top," Josh said without a blink. "See, I knew we could work out everything to our mutual satisfaction," he said, smiling that same lopsided smile that was becoming familiar to her.

"Really?" she answered, walking over to open the front door, giving him a none-too-gentle hint that as far as she was concerned the evening was over. "Then tell me," she asked as he passed by her, "why do I feel like I just landed smack in the middle of an old Doris Day movie?"

Before she could react, Josh leaned down and gave her a quick kiss on the top of her nose. "She has freckles, too," he reminded her. "But Doris is blond. I like your red hair better. See you tomorrow night, Amanda Elizabeth."

She grabbed at his arm to stop him but he was too fast for her and was nearly halfway down the first flight of steps by the time she could stop him by calling out, "We don't leave for Atlantic City until Saturday. Tomorrow's only Friday."

He turned on the stairs to smile up at her, and this time she decided that she didn't like that smile of his at all. "Yes, I know. I stopped by the station today to talk to Vic Harrison and he gave me an itinerary. The crew will pick us up here at seven-thirty Saturday morning, so it seems best if I move here from my hotel Friday night. We don't want to blow the thing before we even get out of the gate, now, do we?"

"Forget it!" Mandy yelled, then quickly lowered her voice before her landlady stuck her head out and poked her nose into things. "You can't stay here overnight," she whispered fiercely. "Mrs. Thorton will have kittens!"

"That ought to get her into the Guinness *Book of Records*," was all Josh said before throwing Mandy a kiss and turning away once more, leaving her standing openmouthed and fuming at the top of the steps.

"Oh what a tangled web we weave, when first, et cetera," Jeanne Tisdale said early the next morning as she watched Mandy pace up and down the small nursery-school office in agitation. "I told you that you should have told the truth at the very beginning, didn't I? What next, Amanda? Do you really think this Joe person is a government agent, or whatever it is you said he was?"

Mandy stopped her pacing and flopped tiredly into a chair. "It sounds as crazy as everything else that's happened, but he did sound sincere. Joe must know that the cameraman he's investigating is the one going along on the trip because he already knows everything else. Lord knows he's entered into the thing heart and soul, going back to the station to talk to Vic Harrison and everything. Oh, I don't know what to think anymore."

"Then let me give you a hint, my dear. *I* think you'd better go shopping," Jeanne reasoned calmly.

"Et tu, Brute?"

"If that means your pseudo-husband agrees with me then I applaud his good sense. Your idea of dressing up, my dear, seems to consist of putting on your best jeans. Do you even own a cocktail dress?"

Mandy did, dozens of them. But she had left them behind when she moved to Allentown, not wanting too many reminders of her past life around to nag her. But she wasn't going to think about that now. "Joe showed more interest in my nightgowns."

Jeanne seemed to consider this for a moment. "I imagine you'll need some sort of demure white peignoir set. You know, breakfast with the newlyweds, that sort of thing."

"Joe prefers black."

"Oh, great."

"That's what I thought. I'll buy one peignoir set just for the cameras, but none of that see-through business. For the rest of the time he'll have to learn to like my Ziggy shirt—and my old bathrobe. After all, it's not like I'm out to impress him, for Pete's sake."

"What hotel are you staying in, Mandy?" Jeanne asked, feeling it was time to change the subject. Amanda was over twenty-one, and her life was her own, no matter how Jeanne felt about it.

"The Tropicana. It's right on the boardwalk. Have you heard of it?"

Jeanne thought for a moment, trying to remember the hotel from her one bus trip to Atlantic City with her mother's church group. "Yes, I remember now. I won twenty dollars there, I think. Of course I lost it again somewhere else. It's a good thing I don't live closer, I can tell you that, because I just can't walk past a slot machine without dropping a quarter in it."

Mandy cringed, shaking her head. "Well, you won't catch me gambling," she vowed fervently. "I think it's silly. Do you think they could afford to build so many casinos, if the people who gambled in them won more than they lost? Besides, standing in some dark, smoky room dropping quarters into a slot and watching a bunch of fruit spin around would bore me out of my skull."

"Famous last words," Jeanne quipped, reaching for the telephone book and searching through it for the number of her favorite dress shop. "I'm going to call Marion for you and tell her you're on your way. Don't worry, her stock isn't limited to polyester. Get at least two dresses for the evenings—definitely one in black to set off your hair—and a couple of simple skirts and blouses for daytime. Charge them to me, and you can pay me back in installments, okay?"

"Yes, mother," Mandy agreed solemnly, knowing better than to fight her friend on the subject. She went around the desk to give Jeanne a hug, then picked up her purse and skipped to the door. "I'll send you a postcard, Jeanne. And I will bet on one sure thing—I'll bet it will be the only one ever sent by a newlywed who writes 'wish you were here!' "

Josh did a little shopping of his own that afternoon, picking up two pairs of swimming trunks, some toiletries and something he never had reason to wear before—pajamas. He had toyed momentarily with the idea of buying a silk pair covered with hearts and Cupid's bows, but he didn't think he could be held responsible for Mandy's reaction, so he settled instead on two plain burgundy silk pajama sets and a matching bathrobe.

Then it was back to WFML and another meeting with his father, who was beginning to ask a few pointed questions.

"I checked with your mother, and she said she hasn't heard from you about your going home," the elder Phillips began clumsily. "Your secretary doesn't know anything, either. So where are you off to, son, some decadent singles cruise in the Caribbean?"

"Dad, I'm thirty-two years old," Josh said, shaking his head in mock sorrow. "I believe I've been a good son—loyal, steadfast, hardworking. So why do you persist in making me into the reincarnation of Don Juan?"

Matt Phillips sat down on the edge of the desk and grinned. "Because it keeps me young, that's why. Besides, your mother and I have been fending off young ladies hungry for your body since you were in the second grade."

"Can I help it if I take after my legendary father?" Josh asked, enjoying his father's flush of embarrassment. "But you've struck out this time. This is strictly business."

"Correct me if I'm wrong, son, but I believe you're in business with *me*. So how come I don't know anything about it?" Matt tried to sound uncaring, but he didn't like this secrecy. Something was in the air, he could smell it, and he didn't like the left-out feeling he had deep in his gut. "Don't you think I can be trusted?"

Josh reached up a hand and rubbed the back of his neck, wincing slightly. "It's not my secret to tell, Dad, I'm sorry. I've just got two favors to ask of you, okay?"

"I'm listening, but I won't give my word until I've heard what you have to say." Suddenly Matt wasn't feeling at all amused.

Josh scribbled a name and address on a slip of paper and passed it to his father. "This first favor is just a small, technical glitch I uncovered the other day. I would handle it myself but I don't have the time. Just tell Vic Harrison, the disc jockey on the afternoon shift, to have a duplicate first-prize stereo and honeymoon trip awarded to the first runner-up in last week's contest. Have him announce it over the air as a tie or something."

"That sounds simple enough. Now let me hear the second favor."

Again Josh wrote something down and handed it to his father. "Here's a telephone number where I can be reached. Please, Dad, don't use it unless there's an emergency. It's a hotel. Ask for Joe Tremaine when you call, and for God's sake don't give your own name if a woman answers the phone."

"You've got that wrong, son. It's 'if a man answers, hang up.'" Matt stared down at the telephone number, then looked up into his son's purposely innocent-looking eyes. "Who the hell is Joe Tremaine?"

"I am, Dad, at least for the next five days."

The older man's eyes narrowed as he struggled to understand. "Are you in some sort of trouble, son?"

Josh gave his neck a last rub. "You might say that, Dad, you might say that. Do you remember a guy named Alexander Tremaine?"

"Alexander Tremaine, Alexander Tremaine," Matt repeated thoughtfully, then looked down at the paper once more. "Joe *Tremaine*. Of course! Now I know why that name sounds so familiar. Lord, that was all so long ago, three, maybe four years. Nasty business." He felt a sinking feeling in his stomach as he remembered Josh's reaction at the time. "Josh, what in blue blazes is going on?"

"Just a little payback, Dad. I've been waiting a long time to see Alex Tremaine brought to his knees. And I think I've finally found just the way to do it."

"Dave Benjamin was a good friend once, Josh, and I know his breakdown threw you. I can understand how you feel, but do you really think even Dave would want you to do this—whatever it is you're planning?"

Josh's face took on a closed expression. "*I* want to do it for Dave. Oh, it's not like I went looking to hurt Tremaine. This just sort of fell into my lap. I can get him, Dad, I know it."

"Legally?"

"Legally, Dad, honest."

"Morally?"

Josh's eyes shifted away from his father's piercing gaze. "Nothing's black and white, Dad, you know that."

"Josh—"

"Hey, look at the time," Josh grabbed his jacket, this time a fine white silk sport coat, and headed for the door. "Gotta run! Give Mom my love when you call her tonight. I'll be in touch."

"*Joshua!*"

Heaving a fatalistic sigh, Josh turned and retraced his steps to stand in front of his father. Matt looked at his son for a long moment, trying to read something in the younger man's eyes. What was he looking for? Anger? The thirst for revenge at any cost? Reckless disregard for anything but his own wants and needs?

Josh's blue eyes stared back levelly, revealing nothing, until at last Matt looked away, waving his hand in dismissal. "Go if you feel you must. But remember this, son, revenge has the tendency to be a double-edged sword. Be careful you don't find yourself ending up as the injured party."

Suddenly, unbidden, a vision of Mandy's guileless face floated in front of Josh's eyes. "Yeah, Dad, I think I'm already figuring that one out for myself. But for reasons that have absolutely nothing to do with Alexander Tremaine, it's too late now to change my plans."

It was nearly ten o'clock and Joe hadn't shown up yet. Mandy let the drapes fall back into place after looking out the window for what must have been the tenth time in as many minutes, and tried hard to be calm. Looking around the living room, she mentally rearranged the small pile of sheets and the pillow she had placed at one edge of the short couch.

Maybe I should make up the couch into a bed before he gets here, she thought, biting her lip. No, that would make it look like I was expecting him. She moved to gather up the bedding and put it back in her bedroom, just as if she wasn't expecting him to show up at all.

"And leave myself wide open to one of his cute comments about where I had planned for him to spend the night," she told herself aloud, dropping the pile of bedding back onto the couch. "No way!"

Giving up her post in the living room, she went through to the bedroom to close her suitcase after giving the contents one last inspection. The black dress Jeanne had suggested lay right on top, carefully wrapped in tissue paper.

"The basic, indispensable black dress," Marion had said as Mandy had gasped at the sight of the low-cut bodice. But it fit so well, the thin spaghetti straps holding it securely to her as the silky material barely skimmed her body from bust to knee.

She had known in an instant that the dress would drive Joe crazy, and that insight had brought a thoughtful smile to her face as she gave in to impulse and declared: "I'll take it!"

But now, standing alone in her bedroom waiting for her pretend husband to show up and bed down on her living-room couch, her earlier bravado deserted her, leaving her wondering just when it was that her normally rational brain had slipped around the bend.

"I must have been out of my mind," she told herself as she impulsively reached for the dress, intent on hanging it in her closet until she could return it to the store. But just as she touched the tissue paper she heard a sharp tattoo on her front door and her hand jerked back as if she had just been stung.

"Oh, Lord, here we go," she breathed, pressing her hands to her suddenly fluttering stomach. Taking a moment to quickly look in the mirror, she saw that she had chewed off all her lipstick in her agitation and reached out for the tube that lay on top of the dresser.

"*Yoohoo* Mandy! Your lover boy is home!"

The open lipstick fell from her hand, breaking neatly in half as it landed on the dresser top. "I'll kill him!" she seethed, running for the door before he said anything else and pulling it open just as he was about to knock once again, this time probably to do his imitation of a rock-and-roll drum solo. "Will you keep your voice down, please," she hissed angrily. "If you wake Mrs. Thor—"

"*Miss Tremaine!*" came a distinctly hostile voice from the bottom of the stairwell. "I thought you understood the house rules. No gentlemen callers after eleven o'clock at night."

"He's not staying, Mrs. Thorton," Mandy called down weakly, stepping down hard on Josh's toes as he opened his mouth to contradict her. "I'm sorry for the noise, honestly. My cousin Harry always was a practical joker. Isn't he a scream?"

"Your cousin?" Mrs. Thorton asked, trying hard to see up the open stairway from the ground floor.

"Cousin Harry," Mandy repeated, trying vainly to pull Josh in from the landing. "Harry—er—Higgenbottom."

"Higgenbottom?" Josh whispered loudly. "There goes that imagination of yours again, Mandy. Anyone else would have said Jones."

"I didn't know you had any relatives," the landlady remarked, putting her slippered foot on the first step.

"Did she think you were hatched from an egg?" Josh stage-whispered, earning himself a killing glance from Mandy.

"Miss Tremaine, it's nearly ten-thirty," Mrs. Thorton called out, just as if she were the town crier announcing the hour. "Tell your Mr. Higgenbottom he must leave soon." They could hear the woman's slippered feet on the stairs as she climbed to the second-floor landing to get a look at Mandy's cousin.

Josh obliged her by leaning over the railing and waving at her. "Hi there, Mrs. Thorton. Hey—nice bathrobe."

The landlady yelped something indistinguishable and, clasping her pink chenille robe tightly across her scrawny breast, hastily made her way back down the stairs. Mandy had to bite down hard on her knuckles to keep from laughing aloud as she heard a door slam shut on the first floor.

"Eleven o'clock?" Josh repeated once they were inside the apartment. "What a wild social life you must lead, Miss Tremaine."

"I manage," she said dismissivly before her eyes widened as she saw the suitcase he held in his left hand. "Did you have to bring that with you? What if Mrs. Thorton had seen it?"

"That's one of the reasons I didn't come over from my hotel until now," he explained as he stepped past her to place the suitcase against the wall. "It was either that or try to convince her that I'm moonlighting as a brush salesman. So, wife," he said, looking around the living room, "ready for bed?"

Mandy took two steps back and looked at him, a knowing sneer on her face. "That's it, make jokes. Go ahead, I'm beginning to get used to them."

"What did I say?" Josh asked blankly. "I'm innocent, I swear it."

"Oh, sure. That's what they all say," Mandy shot back, turning to walk away from him.

"What do they all say? Who are *they*? Where are you going?" She was standing just inside the bedroom, her hand on the doorknob. "Mandy, you're doing it again," he pointed out, shaking his head. "Tell me, do you usually play to the balcony?"

That stopped her in her tracks. "What do you mean? Are you insinuating that I'm putting on *an act*? I suppose you think I have men up here all the time, don't you? Maybe I have three of them hiding in the closet right now, did you think of that? Well, let me tell you, Joe Tremaine, or whatever your name is—"

Josh walked over to her and put his hand under her chin, lifting her face so that she was forced to look at him. "Tut, tut, Doris, sweetheart, you shouldn't carry on so. I promise to be good. You don't have to indulge in another one of your wild flights of fancy to convince me that you're naught but a poor innocent caught up in a web not of your own making."

Mandy looked him up and down, then jerked her chin away from his hand. "Blow it out your ear, buster," she growled. Then, backing up two paces, she gave the door a mighty push, making him jump back before it hit him in the nose.

"I guess this means I'm sleeping on the couch, right?" he called through the heavy door. Then, a satisfied smile on his face, he made his way to the kitchen to get himself a glass of iced tea.

In her bedroom, standing a good three feet away from the door to the living room, Mandy called softly—oh, so softly—"The couch opens up into a bed, Joe. I wouldn't want you to try to sleep on it the way it is or you might wake up with a backache, you poor dear." Then, feeling much, much better about the whole thing, she reached for her Ziggy nightshirt hanging on a hook behind the door.

Chapter Four

Mandy woke slowly, and totally against her will.

Her head remained firmly under her pillow as one hand reached out blindly to grope for the button that would shut off her alarm clock. Reluctantly lifting one corner of her pillow, she opened an eye and tried to focus on the illuminated dial.

"Six o'clock," she groaned, allowing the pillow to fall back into place, fully intending to go back to sleep for at least another three hours before facing the day. It was Saturday, her day off. There wasn't a reason in the world for her to get up at that ungodly hour.

It was quiet again for the space of about ten seconds. Then the pillow went flying through the air to land somewhere near the bottom of the bed as Mandy bolted upright and screeched. "Oh, my God, six o'clock! That only leaves me—" her muddled brain struggled to do the math in her head "—a little over an hour to get ready!"

If only she hadn't lain awake so long the night before, she thought angrily, remembering how her satisfaction at closing the bedroom door in Josh's astonished face had faded when she realized that she had also shut the door on the air conditioner that was humming away in the living-room window. It had been past midnight when the breeze from the open window in her bedroom had finally cooled her enough that she could sleep.

Grabbing up her robe, she went to the door to open it a crack and peek around the corner to see if Josh was still asleep. She wanted to bathe and dress before she had to face him. A small smile escaped her when she looked at the still-closed couch and Josh's masculine form, still wearing the same clothes he had on last night, sprawled half on and half off the cushions. "Tsk, tsk, poor baby," she whispered nastily, her smile widening to a grin.

She locked the bathroom door for the first time in the three years she had lived in the apartment and ran a bath for herself, feeling wonderfully refreshed after a ten-minute soak in her favorite bubble bath. A quick shampoo at the sink took only a few minutes more, as did blow-drying her hair in its casual, chin-length style.

Mandy reached for some lipstick, then reconsidered and took up a bottle of makeup instead. She'd need all her war paint today if she hoped to compete with Josh. Then, slipping back into her bathrobe, she gathered up the toiletries she would need for the trip, slipped them into a plastic bag and walked to the door of the bathroom.

She turned the handle one way, then the other. "It's stuck," she told herself unnecessarily, giving the handle an encouraging jiggle. "It's still stuck," she said, a little louder now. She had to get dressed and finish packing—all preferably before her uninvited guest awoke.

The first stirrings of panic began in her stomach as she closed her eyes and envisioned the camera crew showing up while she was still stuck in the bathroom, clad in her old bathrobe.

"Joe will tell them I'm being a nervous bride again and then they'll all giggle and make jokes at my expense," she informed the door, which remained solidly shut. "Oh, sure, you're on *his* side, aren't you? I'll bet that in French the word door is a masculine noun." Feeling herself to be very much a victim, Mandy then proceeded to give the bottom of the door a swift kick.

"*Ouch!* Oh, darn, darn, darn!" she cried, hopping around the room for a few moments before plopping down on the rug to massage her stinging toes. "I forgot I wasn't wearing shoes."

"You gonna be in there all day?" came a deep voice from the other side of the door. "I picked up the sheets and stashed the evidence in the closet. Now I want to grab a shower and shave. Get a move on, Mandy."

"Typical male," Mandy told the sink as she used it to haul herself to her feet. "Absolutely scintillating in the morning. I'm surprised he hasn't growled for his coffee yet."

"And where's the coffee?" came Josh's complaint, as if on cue. "I can't find a damn thing in that kitchen of yours. Mandy? You are in there, aren't you?" He pressed his ear against the door and heard an unintelligible mumble. "Amanda Elizabeth? Come out, come out, wherever you are."

"I locked the door," Mandy called loudly, cupping her hands around her mouth so that he could hear her through the thick wood. She waited a moment and then knocked loudly on the door with her fist. "Can you hear me out there?"

Josh fairly jumped away from the door grabbing his ear. "They can hear you in downtown Philadelphia, woman," he called back sharply, one hand to his head. "Open the door."

"I already told you—I locked the door," Mandy repeated mulishly. Honestly, she thought, men were so thick!

Josh hadn't slept well. As a matter of fact, he had awakened this morning feeling very sympathetic toward all the pretzels of this world. Also, Josh had not had his morning cup of coffee. His mother would have told Mandy that Josh before coffee was not a pretty sight. Unfortunately, Mandy didn't know Josh's mother.

"Three cheers for you, Mandy, you locked the door. Now *open* it, damn it!" She heard him bellow, and stepped back against the side of the tub, pulling the front of her bathrobe around her for protection.

"I can't," she complained, a slight tremor entering her voice. "The stupid lock is stuck."

About half a minute elapsed, during which Mandy heard a masculine voice muttering and grumbling words she was glad the solid width of the door kept her from understanding. "But then why did you lock the door, Amanda Elizabeth, if you know it gets stuck?" Josh questioned at last employing a tone that Mandy instantly recognized as the one she used when trying to get a three-year-old to tell her why he had put his bologna sandwich in the school aquarium.

Instantly her mood changed from one of anxiety to one of righteous belligerence. "Because I was taking a bath with a possible sex maniac sleeping in the next room, that's why!" she shot back testily.

"Change that to possible *homicidal* maniac, you idiotic—" Josh's impulsive tirade ended abruptly as he suddenly saw the ridiculousness of their situation. If he didn't get that door open soon the crew would be here to pick them up and find his "bride" hiding out in a locked bathroom. "Where's your toolbox?" he called, trying hard to keep his voice calm and conciliatory.

"I don't have a toolbox. I have that screwdriver you used the other night and some other stuff in the drawer next to the sink. What are you going to do?" She heard him moving away from the door. Where had he gone now? "Joe?" She put her head to the door, but couldn't hear anything. "Joe?" she called one more time, feeling somehow deserted.

Suddenly there was a loud crash and an angry yelp coming from the direction of the kitchen. Mandy slapped a hand to her mouth. "Whoops!" she said, grimacing. She had forgotten to tell him that the drawer was broken, and tended to fall if it was pulled out too far. "Joe? What happened?" she asked nervously as she could hear him making strange, strangled noises in the living room.

"That damned drawer fell on my foot, as if you didn't know. You've got this whole place booby-trapped!" he yelled by way of an answer as he sat on the coffee table inspecting his scraped ankle.

"You're paranoid, Joe Tremaine, or whatever the blue blazes your name is!" she yelled back, greatly offended. "Do you know that?"

He stood up and hobbled toward the bathroom door, hammer and screwdriver ready. "After I get these hinges off this miserable door, I am going to proceed to murder you, Amanda Elizabeth Tremaine," he fairly growled. "Just so you know *that!*"

Mandy could hear scraping noises as Josh tried to pry up the paint-encrusted hinges that were, luckily, hung on the outside of the door. She covered her mouth with a towel to hold back her laughter as the absurdity of the whole situation finally hit her. "Golly whiz, you sound a little upset. Does this mean the honeymoon is over, sweet cheeks?" she yelled to him before collapsing against the side of the tub in a helpless fit of the giggles.

Josh sat slouched in the corner of the back seat of the plush navy-blue limousine, silently nursing his wounds. From a poor beginning, the morning had progressed steadily downhill. Once he had succeeded in removing the door of her prison, Mandy had greeted him with a scathing look and an order to replace the door immediately or else she would report him to Mrs. Thorton. Then she had stomped off barefoot to her bedroom to get dressed, leaving him, literally, holding the door.

By the time he had taken a bath—he couldn't remember the last time he had taken one, but he thought he could remember sharing the water with a rubber duck—he was thoroughly miserable and ready for a fight. "Who the hell ever heard of a bathroom without a shower in this day and age?" he had asked accusingly when he finally emerged from the bathroom, three pieces of toilet paper stuck to his nicked chin. "And your mirror is impossible. I could barely see to shave."

Mandy hadn't answered, he remembered now, other than to smile and tell him his coffee was ready and waiting for him on the kitchen counter. It had been cold, too, as if she hadn't planned it that way.

Then the film crew had shown up, ten minutes ahead of schedule and so full of early-morning cheer that he had entertained the thought of slowly strangling all three of them—four, if he counted Mandy, who had greeted them like long-lost cousins.

Chaos had instantly ensued, what with the technician grousing about the lack of electrical outlets for his precious equipment, and the director—some sorry-looking blonde named, of all things, Lois Lamour, and reeking of perfume—fluttering around telling them how "terrifically exciting" it was to be filming in Atlantic City.

"Get me some coffee," Josh had said to Mandy when he could get her attention.

"I did get you some already, darling," she had chirped, wifelike, smiling at the cameraman, who had been inspecting her through the opening made by his cupped hands as he held them out in front of him like a camera lens.

"But it's cold, *sweetheart*," Josh had returned, smiling at the cameraman as he spoke through gritted teeth.

He never had gotten his coffee, he remembered now, looking across the expanse of the wide back seat at his pretend wife. Mandy was sitting primly in her corner, talking to the director, who was perched on one of the jump seats like an overage canary.

His eyes narrowing thoughtfully, he remembered Mandy's prediction that God was getting her for thinking about doing something wrong. Was it possible Josh was being punished for what he was about to do? He'd have to think about that; it was beginning to seem possible.

"Have you been directing long, Lois?" Mandy was asking as the limousine purred its way along the Atlantic City Expressway. "It seems so glamorous."

Lois—looking to be about thirty-five but trying to look twelve—patted her bony chest and boasted: "I've been at WFML for three years now," she said proudly. "Perhaps you've seen the *Cousin Susie Show*?"

"That cute little program with the woman dressed up like someone in *Hansel and Gretel*?" Mandy asked, seemingly delighted. "The one where the little children get to sit around on those adorable pink and blue toadstools and listen to stories? And Cousin Susie sings songs she's written herself while she accompanies herself on the accordion?" Gag me, Mandy thought, that's the *worst* show on television. She flashed Lois a brilliant smile. "I just adore that show! Do you mean that you direct that darling program?"

Lois beamed, thrilled to have her talent recognized. "I even produced it. Oh, yes, that one was my baby, start to finish," she admitted modestly, an unbecoming blush reddening her sallow skin. "I'm also the director for the weather segment of the evening news, you know. I only hope my stand-in can handle it while I'm gone."

Oh, so Lois Lamour was responsible for the weather segment, was she? Josh thought evilly, feeling like it was time he got a little of his own back. Sitting forward, he leaned over a bit to gain the director's attention. "That's a good show, Lois," he told her, earning himself a smile from the woman. The smile faded, however, as he added, "That's why it's such a pity about the weather girl. Gee, if only you could ditch that dame. What a dog. I mean, she's a real bowwow, isn't she?"

"That's my sister, Lana," Lois replied, her bottom lip jutting out dangerously. "I handpicked her myself. The name Lana Lamour *means* weather, in Allentown!"

Mandy was instantly all conciliation. Placing a hand on Josh's forearm, she dug her nails into his bare flesh. "Oh dear, my Joe is such a tease, isn't he, Lois? He was just being silly." She turned to glare at Josh, who was sitting there, his blue eyes as wide and innocent-looking as a choirboy's on Christmas morning. "You were just being silly, weren't you, Joe, dear?"

"I was?" he asked, blinking twice. "Oh, yes, of course." He looked away from Mandy, who was staring daggers at him, and directed his cherubic gaze on Lois. "I was only being silly, Lois," he recited dutifully. "I really like the weather girl." Seeing that the director was hardly looking mollified, he pressed on, "Hey, I *love* that weather girl. I've always had a thing for big hips in plaid. As a matter of fact—"

"Joe feels rather strange about this honeymoon, Lois," Mandy broke in before Josh could say anything more. "You know how men are, always nervous about anything that's considered even remotely romantic. It embarrasses them, makes them feel their macho image is threatened or something. You'll have to excuse him," she ended, increasing the pressure of her hand until he responded.

"Yes, Lois," he said quickly in self-defense, using his left hand to pry Mandy's fingers off his right forearm, and then lifting her hand to his lips as if to prove she was wrong, even if he was willing to humor her. "I guess this whole television thing is going to take a little getting used to. Mandy entered the contest without seeking my consent, you know, and I really don't know if I like how it's going so far. I mean—having our honeymoon filmed for television. It's so—so *public*, you know."

"But we just *love* the stereo, don't we, honeybun," Mandy put in hastily, seeing that Lois was beginning to look even more cranky.

"Yes, where was the stereo?" the director asked, momentarily diverted. "We should have gotten some film of it. We'll have to do it when we get back. You know, I don't think I remember seeing it in the living room."

"No, no, you didn't, did you?" Josh put in as Mandy started showing signs of panic. Here was his chance to pay her back for the cold coffee, and petty as it seemed, he wasn't about to let the opportunity slip by unnoticed. "That's because it's in our bedroom. Right beside the white bearskin rug." He turned to Mandy, running a finger down the length of her throat and enjoying the slight wiggle of her body as she reacted to the shivers his teasing stroke had caused. "You read my wife's winning entry, didn't you, Lois? Need I say more?"

Look at him, Mandy thought wretchedly. His smile is positively obscene, she told herself, wishing she could crawl into a hole and pull it in after her.

Chuck, the technician, who was still grumbling about trying to work around an inadequate electrical supply, perked up his ears from the front seat. "Yeah, I heard about that from Vic. It was a real scorcher, Lois. Vic said he could barely read it on the air."

"It was not! He could so!" Mandy protested, looking back and forth between Chuck and her "husband" while the two men smiled, one knowingly, the other with smug satisfaction. Joe had said he was going to try to get a copy of her letter, and it would appear he had succeeded. "It— it was a *lovely* letter. Romantic. You make it all sound so—so sordid!"

The cameraman, who went by the highly innocuous name of Herb, looked up from the light meter he was checking and asked, "What did it say, Chuck? I must have missed it."

Joe looked over at Mandy, who was glaring at him in helpless rage and embarrassment, and waggled his eyebrows at her. "I think I just might have a copy in my coat, Herb," he said helpfully. "You want me to show it to you?"

"I'll order a huge pot of hot coffee every morning from room service the moment you wake up," Mandy promised rashly in an undertone. "And I won't lock another bathroom door ever again."

Josh looked at her for a long moment, deciding whether or not he felt satisfied. "Drop the 'honeybun' business and you've got yourself a deal," he bargained quietly, reaching for his coat, which was draped over the other jump seat.

"Done," Mandy promised, then sighed in relief as Josh searched through his coat pockets before apologizing to Herb.

"Can't seem to find it. Sorry, fella," he said, leaning back once more and sliding an arm around Mandy's shoulders. "But take my word for it, it was a great letter. Hey," he added, looking out the window, purposely changing the subject, "I think we're almost there. Lois, did you say the Tropicana is right on the boardwalk?"

As the director pulled a brochure out of her briefcase and began reading aloud about the hotel, Mandy leaned closer to look up into Josh's face and whisper, "Truce?"

Josh looked down at her, seeing the apprehension in her innocent green eyes. Apprehension, and something else. Unless he missed his guess, Amanda Elizabeth Tremaine liked him in spite of herself. He suppressed a wince as his guilty conscience gave him a sharp poke right between the shoulder blades.

What had started as a joke—a mad lark aimed at easing his boredom by spending a few days romancing a beautiful, if slightly kooky, woman—had quickly mushroomed into a chance to revenge an old hurt. And while one part of him told him he had every right to do what he was doing, another part of him knew he would probably end up hurting this innocent girl along the way.

He had to keep it light, keep their relationship strictly on the surface. Mandy was better off fighting with him than she was believing he was one of the good guys. "Truce?" he repeated, leaning down to whisper in her ear. "Not by the hair of my chinny-chin-chin, sweetheart."

Watching as her green eyes clouded over with pain, Josh was at a loss to explain why he suddenly felt more than a little injured himself.

The Concierge suite at the Tropicana was everything Mandy had expected, and quite a bit more. It was on two levels, for one thing, consisting of a formal sitting room that connected with the bedroom area by way of a spiral staircase. With the couch on one floor and the king-size bed on another, Mandy could see no reason for any problems, if only Joe would promise to behave himself.

He had been reasonably cooperative so far, she reminded herself as she walked around the two-level suite, admiring the floral carpets and inspecting what looked to be original oil paintings hanging in a cluster above the couch. She had already unpacked, claiming two drawers of the dresser and one of the closets as her own before Josh had so much as come up the steps to inspect the bedroom.

Once he did, however, the large room suddenly seemed suffocatingly small, and Mandy escaped to the lower level, babbling something about wanting to read the guest information booklet she had seen lying on the coffee table.

Wait until he sees the bathroom, she thought, standing in front of the huge wall of windows that overlooked the boardwalk. A person could float a battleship in that tub. Not that Joe would think that. Oh, no, he'll probably make some ridiculous suggestion about bathing together to save water or something like that.

"Don't go looking for trouble, Mandy," she warned herself aloud. "Just because he's refused to call a truce doesn't mean he's just been waiting for the film crew to leave so he can jump your bones. Most of the time he acts like he doesn't even like you, for heaven's sake."

She walked over to the credenza to inspect the cleverly arranged fruit tray the hotel management had sent up along with a complimentary bottle of wine. "Have an apple, Mandy," she suggested, inspecting the huge pyramid of fruit from several angles until she decided what she wanted to try first. "Maybe an apple a day will keep the bully away."

"Ah, yes, Amanda Elizabeth, but will it keep the wolf away?" She heard the amused voice coming from the direction of the stairs just as her fingers made contact with the big, red apple she had chosen. She whirled around sharply, startled by the sound of his voice, the apple in her hand. Unfortunately, her movement jostled the half dozen other apples, the two bunches of grapes (one green, one red), the small bunch of bananas, the oranges, the pears, the plums and even the small bottles of gourmet preserves tucked up with the rest of the fruit that remained on the tray.

"Oh, look what you made me do!" she accused as the fruit went tumbling to the floor, one of the freed oranges coming to rest at Josh's feet. "Do you have to sneak up on a person like that?"

"I do not *sneak up* on people. I walk into rooms like any other normal person. It's not my fault if you were so busy talking to yourself that you didn't hear me."

"Then you admit that you were eavesdropping?" Clearly, she had decided that, where Josh was concerned, the best defense was a good offense. "Silly question. Of course you do. Why else would you sneak up on me like that, if it wasn't because you're one of those weirdos that gets their kicks listening in on private conversations."

Josh's shoulders shook with silent laughter at Mandy's last words. "Just having a little Mandy-to-Mandy chat, were you? Did you ever consider outside help? Talking to yourself, feelings of paranoia—" he shook his head. "I don't know, Amanda Elizabeth, I just don't know."

"At least I don't think I'm James Bond and Don Juan and—and Soupy Sales, all rolled into one," Mandy sniped. "Oh, never mind. Just cough or something next time you come up behind me like that."

"How about a fanfare of trumpets?" he suggested, bending down to pick up the orange before walking over to stand in front of Mandy. "Yours, I believe."

Mandy snatched the orange out of his hand and angrily slammed it down on the silver tray which, since she had hit it on one corner, immediately flipped into the air like a giant silver tiddlywink before doing a graceful swan dive to the floor, giving Joe's sore ankle a glancing blow on its way down. "Damn it all to hell, woman," he swore, falling to the carpet at her feet, "are you trying to kill me?"

Mandy just went on picking up the fallen fruit and piling it on the fallen tray.

"Well? Are you?" Josh repeated, looking across at her downcast head.

She looked up, blinking her wide green eyes twice, as if in confusion. "Oh. You wanted an answer? Sorry. I had assumed it to be a rhetorical question."

Josh narrowed his eyes and made a respectful grimace. He should have realized he had been pushing too hard, baiting her as he had all day. "Touché, Amanda. Message received and acknowledged. I guess I've been coming on a little too strong today, huh?"

"Do the words 'Mack truck' ring a bell with you?"

"Only a truck? Surely you mean a steamroller?" He put out his hand to keep Mandy from reaching for the bunch of green grapes. "I was doing it for your own good, you know."

She sat back on her heels, looking at him in amazement. "Of course you were," she said with a sneer. "As a rule, I've always found being embarrassed, insulted and maligned—in between bouts of having my virtue assaulted—to be quite character building. Thank you, Joe, thank you very much." She jerked her arm away, picked up the last of the fruit and stood up to put the tray back on the table.

Josh scrambled to his feet before she could reach the stairway. "Hey, come back here. You don't understand what I mean. I didn't want to bring this up but—how can I say this without sounding like some kind of conceited ass? Look, Amanda, this whole thing started out as a lark, right? A little innocent impersonation to help the nursery school."

"Wrong," she countered, putting her foot on the first step. "It started out as me showing up to admit my deception to Vic Harrison. I've been cast in a supporting role ever since I stepped into that darned freight elevator. And another thing—"

Josh threw up his hands, as if begging for silence. "All right, all right, the whole thing is my fault. I took advantage of your dilemma to further my—er, my investigation of WFML, didn't I? Spare me a recitation of my sins, okay? And come back down here. I don't like having to crane my neck to talk to you."

"Why not? I have to do it to talk to you. Turnabout is fair play," Mandy said nastily, but she did come back down and stand in front of him, her arms militantly folded across her chest. "Okay, Joe," she commanded, general to underling. *"Talk to me."*

He looked down into those damned innocent green eyes and felt his stomach sink to his toes. He'd rather take candy from a baby—or a hungry grizzly bear. How could he tell her he was trying to be every kind of rotter he could think of in order to keep her from becoming infatuated with him?

Worse, how could he tell her she had to remain immune to him or else he, who was becoming more captivated with Mandy of the green eyes, fiery red hair and adorable freckles, couldn't be held responsible for the consequences once the two of them were alone in the hotel room for the night ... for the next four nights.

"Well? I'm still waiting. Speak, oh oracle."

Josh closed his eyes for a moment, racking his brain for an easy way to say what must be said. "I don't want you to like me too much," he blurted out at last, just as Mandy had given a frustrated sigh and turned away from him.

If nothing else, Josh's words accomplished two things. One, they stopped Mandy dead in her tracks, and two, they succeeded in getting him her undivided attention. Slowly, she turned on her heels to face him. Slowly, her gaze traveled from his face to his toes and then back up to his face. Slowly, a small smile formed on her features.

"You overestimate yourself, Joe," she said finally, just as he thought she was either going to laugh in his face or deliver a sharp slap to his cheek. "I may dress like a teenager, as you say, but I gave up impossible teenage crushes long ago. You may credit yourself with leaving a string of broken hearts all across this country, God knows you've got the ego for it—not to mention the wardrobe—but you needn't lose sleep over the state of my heart. Buster, I wouldn't take you on a bet!''

With that, Mandy walked leisurely toward the stairway and carefully watched her step as she climbed to the balcony bedroom. After a few moments Josh heard the soft closing of the bathroom door and finally let out the breath he had been holding for what had seemed to be forever.

''I think she took that fairly well, considering,'' he told the oil portrait over the side table. ''My God,'' he then exclaimed, shaking his head in disbelief as he realized he had just talked out loud to himself. ''Now she's got me doing it!'' Evading the condemning eyes—or so they looked to him—that stared at him from the portrait, he left the room, going off in search of a dark, quiet cocktail lounge where he could collect his thoughts before he and Mandy met the television crew for a late lunch.

Upstairs, Mandy, who had been standing just inside the bathroom trying to decide whether she should return to the bedroom, pack her things and then hop the next bus back to Allentown, heard the loud slam of the door as Josh left. Crossing to stand before the mirror hanging above the oversize vanity, she carefully inspected her reflection, looking for the crack in her composure that had led Josh to believe she was capable of making a fool of herself over him.

Did her eyes look the least bit dreamy? No, she decided, peering at herself intently. Was there an unnatural flush to her cheeks? None that she could discern. So what had he seen to make him think she was, to put it crudely, getting the hots for him?

"Maybe I look desperate," she suggested aloud. "Old-maid nursery-school teacher befriended by playboy investigator makes nuisance of herself by throwing her love-starved body at him. No," she decided, dismissing the idea. "For one thing, it's too long to make a good headline, even in one of the gossip newspapers. Besides, who does he think he is, some sort of pagan love god, irresistible to women? I should have told him that love gods aren't royal pains in the butt first thing in the morning, that's what I should have told him. And I should have reminded him that he was the one who kissed me in the elevator, not the other way around."

The more Mandy talked to herself, the madder she got, with both Josh, who was so unspeakably arrogant as to think she would fall for him, and with herself, who she darn well knew to be capable of liking him more than she should. He could be so nice, she thought, then wondered if it was his niceness or his contrariness that most attracted her to him.

Even their fights had pleased her, she remembered as she deliberately ran a foot-deep bath for herself, using a generous hand with the bubble bath she had brought with her. It was only when he tried to kiss her that she pulled back, feeling faint stirrings of danger.

Just as she was dipping her toes in the water, testing its warmth, a silly thought struck her. "If he doesn't want me to become too involved with him, he should *chase* me, not *fight* with me. He's going about this thing all wrong!"

The bathwater was just right, and she immersed herself up to her chin, sighing with combined contentment and the realization that she knew something Josh didn't know.

"And *I'm* not about to tell him," she told the handful of bubbles she had scooped up to hold in front of her. "I'm not going to say a single, solitary word that would help that skunk one bit!" Feeling much better about everything, Mandy blew hard at the bubbles, sending them floating lazily into the air.

Chapter Five

"We won't be needing you at all for the remainder of the day," Lois was telling Josh and Mandy as the waiter handed the five of them menus at the hotel's Brasserie restaurant. "Chuck and Herb have to check out the sound and lighting while I hunt around for some good locations."

"I saw that load of equipment, Chuck," Josh said, turning to the technician who was donning his reading glasses to get a better look at the menu. "I couldn't believe the limo's trunk could possibly have held it all. Was that a videotape machine I helped lift out for you? Some of the controls reminded me of my VCR at home."

"It's a portable playback machine," Chuck replied, always happy to share his knowledge with an interested amateur. "We can watch the screen to see how the setup looks even as we're filming, then use it to review what we've filmed."

"Then you send the videotapes back to the station, ready to go? It's as easy as that?" Josh couldn't believe it would be that simple, and having quick access to the tapes in their completed form fitted in so well with his plans. "That's great."

"It's not quite that cut and dried," Lois corrected, glad to show off in front of the man who had insulted her beloved sister Lana. "We'll be interviewing both of you for about an hour each sometime in the next few days, so that we can use it on the voice-over of the edited tapes. I'll narrate, of course, and your voices will be used during some scenes, but sometimes the viewer will see it as if you or Mandy were actually narrating the action."

"Interview us?" Mandy had picked up at least part of Lois's explanation. "Separately?" She turned her fearful eyes to Josh. "Do we want that? I mean—*separately*?"

Clearly Mandy was worrying that, once separated, they wouldn't be able to keep their stories straight when they answered Lois's questions. Josh hesitated a moment, wondering if this would be another good time to say something bound to set Mandy's back up, but her pleading expression stopped him. "I don't know, Lois," he said, consideringly. "As this is a honeymoon piece, sort of special, you know, perhaps it would be best if Mandy and I could be interviewed together—sort of play off one another, I think I've heard it called."

Surprisingly, it was Herb, the cameraman, who cast the deciding vote. "Sounds good to me," he said, never taking his eyes from the menu in front of him. "Save a hell of a lot of time, too."

"You have other plans, Herb?" Mandy slid in before Lois could open her mouth to argue. "Perhaps you want to work on your tan? I know I do. I feel so pale, even if it is the middle of August.''

Josh pressed his fingers to the bridge of his nose and closed his eyes, as if in pain. Oh, no, Mandy was playing detective, and they hadn't even been in Atlantic City three hours. Not only that, but now she was looking at him as if to say, "Well, aren't you going to jump in and ask a few questions of your own now that I've opened the door for you?''

He'd better keep up his end, he thought, racking his brain for a question he could ask. "Will you guys be getting any free time?'' He directed his question to Lois, who seemed eager to talk.

"Oh, my, I really doubt it,'' she said, earning herself a snort of derision from Chuck, who clearly thought differently. "Five days may seem like a long time to you, Joe, but today is half gone already and the last day will be mostly concerned with loading our gear for the return to Allentown. That only leaves us three days and four nights in which to do the actual filming.''

"Depending on the director,'' Chuck said to Josh in an aside.

"I imagine the cameraman is terribly important,'' Mandy pushed, giving Josh a meaningful kick under the table. "I mean, the whole thing would be pointless if the cameraman wasn't able to capture exactly what the director wanted.''

Herb looked at Mandy, his rather thin face devoid of expression. "Yeah,'' he said shortly, then looked around for the waiter. "How does a guy get a drink around here?''

Bless you, Herb, Josh thought silently, as he had secretly feared that their cameraman might be a Perrier man. The jig would have been up even before it started if Herb had been a teetotaler. "You shouldn't make a thirsty man talk until he's had a chance to wet his whistle, darling," he told Mandy, who just shrugged off his implied warning.

"Yes, let's eat, drink and be merry," Lois chirped happily, having already decided on the strip steak. "We have five glorious days of expense-account eating ahead of us, folks, so we might as well take advantage of it."

Dad will be tickled pink to hear how his loyal employees view their fringe benefits, Josh mused ruefully, as all three WFML employees ordered lavishly from the menu. "How about you, Mandy," he asked, seeing her frown as she read the prices. "Might as well take advantage of it, like Lois says. What will you have—or should I order for you?"

Not really wanting the chopped sirloin, which was the cheapest thing she could see that even mildly appealed to her, she agreed to let Josh order for her, hoping against hope he wouldn't order strawberries, which made her break out in a rash all over her body.

"How could you do that to me!"

The door had just closed on the television crew and Mandy turned to attack. "Do what?" Josh asked innocently, moving away to turn on the television set in the corner of the room.

"Do what? Do what?" she repeated in a mocking singsong voice. "How could you order me *well-done* steak, that's what! It was like shoe leather!"

"It was not," he contradicted, flipping through the channels to find the sports network. "I had the same thing you did and it was delicious. You just aren't used to eating civilized food, that's all."

"And I had to eat it, didn't I? It was either that or let Lois and the rest of them know that my dearest 'husband' doesn't have even the faintest idea as to how I like my steak cooked." Mandy stomped over to the couch and threw herself down in a huff. "I know what you were doing, you know."

Josh turned to peer at her inquisitively. "You do, do you?"

"Yes, mister smarty-pants, I do."

Mandy was marvelous in a fury. Her eyes seemed to flash emerald fire, and her freckled face took on an animation that brought out all of Josh's latent caveman cravings. "Well, why don't you run your theory by me, just to show me how smart you are?"

"No!" She wanted to sulk, she wanted to make him suffer. But when he smiled, something inside her snapped. Sitting up straight on the couch, her legs tucked beneath her as if she were a cat, ready to spring, she rose to his bait. "All right, I'll tell you. You were punishing me for trying to learn something about Herb. You remember Herb, don't you? The guy you told me you were here to investigate? What's the matter? Didn't you think I could even ask him a simple question without giving the game away?"

"You're feeling insulted, aren't you, Amanda Elizabeth?" Josh deduced maddeningly. "Poor baby. How can I make it up to you?" He furrowed his forehead, as if deep in thought. "I know!" he announced, beaming at her cheerfully. "I'll go down to the hotel shops and buy you a trench coat. Would you like a thirty-eight special, too?" He seemed to be considering the idea. "No," he said quickly, as Mandy's eyes seemed to shoot daggers at him, "I don't think you'd look good in a shoulder holster. It'd give you bulges in all the wrong places. I like your bulges where they are now."

Jumping to her feet, Mandy began pacing rapidly around the room, her arms flapping like the wings of a flightless bird in her agitation. "That's right, make jokes. Ha, ha, very funny. You ought to go on the stage, Joe whatever-your-name-is, you know that? You could bill yourself as the Obnoxious Comic. You couldn't be another Unknown Comic, because that would mean you'd have to put a paper bag over your head, and heaven knows your immense ego couldn't stand that! Oh, no, you'd—"

Josh cut off her tirade by going up to her and physically trapping her arms at her sides. "You're getting hysterical again, Mandy, just like in the elevator," he told her as she tried to wriggle out of his grasp.

"So? What are you going to do about it, big man? Give me that tired old 'that's how they do it in Hollywood' line again? Check that idea of mine about your being a comedian. You don't have any original material."

The movement of her body against his chest was making a mockery of all his good intentions. "Oh, yeah, wife? That's what you think," he gritted, giving her no time to respond as he bent down and effortlessly hoisted her into his arms. In three quick strides he was beside the couch, and the two of them landed on the soft cushions a second later, Mandy clinging tightly to his neck as he followed her down. "How's this for innovative thinking?" he asked before capturing her mouth with his own.

All Josh's resolutions, all his good intentions, flew out the window with his first real taste of Mandy. She was sweetness; she was fire; she was as intoxicating and addicting as strong drink. His mouth moved over hers; his lips drank from hers; his tongue tasted hers. As her body moved under him, first in protest, and then in passion, he felt his skin being scorched even through his clothes. He wanted more, still more. He wanted it all—everything she was willing to give.

And she was giving, giving and taking with all the passion her red hair and fiery nature allowed. She was lost, and had been from the first moment she felt his body molded so tightly against her own. All her resolutions, all her very natural reservations, fled unlamented as she gave herself up to her first encounter with the rapture of being held in a lover's embrace.

"You drive me crazy, lady," Josh confessed when at last his good sense made an appearance, his forehead pressed against hers as they both struggled to regain their breath.

Mandy looked up into the eyes scant inches from her own, so close that she could clearly see her reflection in their deep blue centers. What had happened? Could that abandoned-looking female really be her? It didn't seem possible. Clearly she had better get this situation back under control. "I drive you crazy?" she quipped, turning her head away. "I'd be flattered, if I didn't know that it's such a short trip."

His maddening lopsided grin came into view as Josh slowly disengaged himself from Mandy and slid to one side to end up in a sitting position on the flowered carpet. "You have a great recovery time, darling," he told her admiringly, running a noticeably shaky hand through his dark hair. "Unfortunately, I can't say the same for myself. I'm sure you'll excuse me if I leave you here alone for a while."

"Where—where are you going?" Mandy asked anxiously as Josh got up and started across the room, her face flushing a deep pink as she saw that somehow his shirttail had gotten loose and she had the sinking feeling that she might have had a lot to do with its escape.

"I'm going to take a shower," Josh growled. "A cold shower."

She watched him until his legs disappeared up the top of the stairs, then sat up, guiltily straightening her wrinkled skirt and blouse. "Good thought," she mused aloud. Then she spied the complimentary bottle of wine, still cooling in the ice bucket and, although she rarely drank, decided it was as good a time as any for a medicinal dose of alcohol.

Mandy stood quietly before the huge windows in the living room, entranced by the sight of the sun coming up over the Atlantic Ocean. She longed to be outside, on the sandy beach, perhaps even astride a horse, galloping through the fringes of the surf. It had been so long, so very long.

Closing her eyes, she could imagine the smells of the sea and the sand, feel the caress of the wind as it blew against her cheeks and tangled in her hair. Was it really more than three years since she had ridden innocently along the beach on her mare, Emma, believing herself to be living in the best of all possible worlds?

A single tear escaped her dark lashes, to roll unheeded down her cheek, and she was startled when a masculine finger appeared to gently sweep it away. "Sunrise melancholia?" Josh asked in a rough whisper, sending a pleasurable shiver down her spine.

Mandy pulled back sharply from the human contact, afraid that if she let herself go, she would launch herself into his arms and bawl like an abandoned child. "Sunrise in the eyes," she corrected pertly, sniffling delicately before allowing the drapery to fall back into place, once more shrouding the living room in semidarkness. "I ordered coffee from room service, just as I promised you I would, my lord. A full pot. It should be here soon, if you want to shower first."

Josh knew when he was being put off, but he decided not to push her—at least not yet. "Sounds great, wife," he told her, dropping his role of hopeful comforter. "You know, I think I could get used to this kind of service." After dropping a quick, husbandly kiss on the side of her cheek, he turned to go upstairs. "But I'll tell you one thing—that couch has got to go."

"If that couch goes, you go with it," Mandy rallied lightly, looking at him fully for the first time and realizing that he was still in his pajamas and bathrobe. "You look like an ad for *Esquire* magazine in that getup."

"A lot you know, my little innocent," he countered, raising his eyebrows a fraction. "I think I look more like an ad for *Playboy*, myself."

Mandy pretended to consider this for a moment, then shook her head. "Naw. You'd have to have a semiclad blonde draped on each arm to look like an ad for *Playboy*."

"Now I'd *really* like to know how you'd know that."

Pretending to take umbrage at his question, Mandy replied firmly, "I don't live my entire life at the nursery school, reading 'Humpty Dumpty.' I do know a little something about the real world."

Josh ran his gaze over her shiny-clean, makeup-free face, then down over her white cotton knit shirt, faded denim skirt and strapped low-heeled sandals. "Yes, you do, don't you? As in *very* little. And you know what? I think I like that about you the best of all."

After watching Josh disappear up the stairs to take his shower, Mandy turned back to the window, pretending to enjoy the sunrise, but her eyes were closed against the pain she felt clutch at her chest at Josh's words. If he only knew how much she really understood about the workings of the real world, she thought fatalistically, he'd run from her like a man running for his life—like she'd been running for her life for over three years.

She stared sightlessly at the scenery, deliberately blocking out her thoughts by concentrating on the events of the previous evening. After a congenial late dinner with the television crew in the hotel's Regent Court restaurant, Mandy had pleaded a headache and she and Josh had declined Lois's offer to take in one of the shows in the casino in favor of an early night.

Even in the clear light of day, Mandy winced at the remembrance of the sly winks exchanged between Lois and Chuck just before Josh led her to the banks of elevators in the lobby.

Little did they know that Mandy had been in bed, and very much alone, not more than twenty minutes later, with Josh lying stretched out on the living-room couch, watching the New York Mets pulverize the St. Louis Cardinals while he sipped on a cold beer he had ordered from room service.

Mandy had been surprised at Josh's easy cooperation, she remembered now, surprised and, if she was going to be truthful with herself, just the tiniest bit disappointed. After their rather passionate interlude on the couch she had been looking forward to the evening with mixed anxiety and anticipation.

But Josh was doing the right thing—keeping it light. He was a fair man, she decided, and he was making no bones about the fact that once the honeymoon and his investigation were over he planned to walk away from her, heart-whole and guilt-free.

At least he was being flattering about it, letting her know that he was attracted to her, even if it was only a physical attraction. After all, what else could it be, she reasoned sadly, considering the fact that he didn't hide his opinion that she didn't really have both her oars in the water. People don't fall in love with people they see as hysterical, melodramatic or juvenile, and Josh had called her all of those, and more.

"He's not exactly my fantasy prince come riding into my life on his snow-white stallion, either," she explained ruefully to the rising sun. "He's rude, arrogant, conceited, a terrible tease—and much too secretive. Why, I don't believe I really even like him, even if he does have the sexiest blue eyes I've ever seen." She was silent for a moment, thinking. "Even if he has the cutest smile that goes all the way up into his eyes."

She walked over to the corner and pulled on the cord that opened the drapes. "Even if he makes me laugh, and can make me madder than anyone I've ever met, it doesn't mean a thing." Sitting down in one of the wing-back chairs, she raised a hand and began worrying one knuckle with her teeth. "Even if his kisses turn my whole world inside out and his body—oh, damn, that must be the coffee!"

The firm rapping on the door of the suite interrupted Mandy's musings just as, or so she thought, she might have been getting somewhere, and she opened the door reluctantly, a rather forbidding frown on her face.

"*Good* morning!" the waiter exclaimed cheerily, carrying in a heavy silver tray and placing it on the coffee table with a theatrical flourish. "Isn't it a glorious day?"

Mandy looked at the waiter, a small, dark-haired youth about her own age. He had the whitest teeth and the widest grin she had ever seen. He also looked like he didn't have a care in the world. Mandy's frown deepened. It wasn't fair that this man could be so happy when she was so miserable.

The waiter's smile faded slightly, then spread across his face once more. "Hey, you're the newlyweds who won that contest, aren't you?" he asked, snapping his fingers as if he'd just remembered that fact. "I saw the film crew come in with you yesterday. What a break for you guys. I'm an actor, you know, even if I am wearing this uniform. If I had known I could get television exposure as easily as you have, I'd have dragged my girlfriend Sylvia off to City Hall in a flash. I'm Rollie, by the way, Rollie Estrada. I'm going to change it, though, 'cause of that Eric guy, you know. Too confusing for the masses otherwise."

His enthusiasm was infectious, and Mandy found she was smiling in spite of herself.

"That's the ticket!" Rollie encouraged, seeing the change in her mood. "This could be your big break, you know, if you work it right. With that red hair and those great legs, hey, you could be the next Lucy. Can you take a pratfall?"

Mandy screwed up her face in confusion. "A pratfall. I'm not sure. What is it?"

Rollie held up one finger as if to say, "Just one second, I'll be right with you," and ran lightly across the room and up several steps of the spiral staircase. He turned to face the room and paused for a moment to straighten his jacket, then adjust his facial expression, and with a few quick hand movements he assumed an air of sophisticated elegance. Head held high, he then began his descent, before seeming to slip on the third step from the bottom and, a hilarious look of astonishment widening his expressive eyes, he somersaulted comically down the remainder of the stairs, coming to rest at Mandy's feet.

"Oh, Rollie, are you hurt?" Mandy asked quickly, but before she could reach down to help him, the waiter hopped to his feet, his toothy grin back in place.

"*That's* a pratfall," he announced, glowing. "Pretty good, huh? You should see me when I'm really warmed up."

Above their heads, Mandy could hear the sound of running feet, and within seconds Josh was racing down the stairs, a huge bath sheet wrapped around him from his waist to his ankles, his face covered neck to nose with a heavy coating of shaving cream. "Mandy!" he shouted as the turning of the staircase had his back to the room. "I heard you fall. Are you all right, honey?"

Mandy opened her mouth to answer him, but suddenly Josh lost his own footing, and within the blinking of an eye he was somersaulting down the last three stairs, doing a grand imitation of Rollie, if only he knew it. He, too, landed at Mandy's feet, shaving cream now smeared all over his face and sticking to his chest and shoulders. She could see the small crystal beads of water that still clung to his back and legs after his shower.

"Oh, Joe," she wailed, falling to her knees to run her hands over his bare upper body, praying he hadn't broken anything. "Are you all right?"

"Never mind me, damn it. My feet were still wet and I slipped." He grabbed her arms and began inspecting her for injuries. "Are *you* all right? That's the only thing that's important."

He was so serious, so very concerned, that it tugged on Mandy's heartstrings. Unfortunately, with his smeared shaving cream, mussed wet head and towel-clad body sprawled inelegantly, if modestly, on the flowered rug, he was also the funniest thing Mandy had seen in years.

She couldn't help it. Even though she knew she was courting disaster, she sat back on her heels and began to laugh. Worse, she then put one hand to her mouth, unknowingly dotting it with the shaving cream that had gotten on her when she had touched him, and used the other hand to point at him, wordlessly telling him exactly what she found to be so amusing.

Josh wrinkled his brow, trying to understand. "What's so funny?" he asked, a question that sent Mandy into another attack of the giggles, and she rolled onto the floor, nearly howling with mirth. "Damn it, Mandy, what's so funny?"

She tried to speak. "You thought...and then you...oh, you look so *funny*! I didn't . . . it was him," she said between bouts of laughter, tears now streaming down her cheeks while the white cream around her mouth made her look like a mad dog.

"Who him? Him who?" Josh looked up, suddenly aware that they were not alone. Rollie, who had been trying to melt into the background, gave Josh a wincing grin and a jaunty salute. "Who the hell are you?" Josh exploded, rising to his feet and dragging the towel around his middle more securely.

Using all of her strength to compose herself before Josh bit poor Rollie's head off, Mandy scampered to her feet and took her supposed husband by the arm. "He's Rollie Estrada, although he's going to change his name so nobody mistakes him for that Eric guy. You have to admit, those white teeth might confuse some people."

Josh closed his eyes and counted to ten. He had been right: God *was* getting him.

"Anyway, Rollie's going to be an actor, you see," Mandy pressed on, her words tumbling over themselves as she used her free hand to wipe the shaving cream from her upper lip. "And he thought I might be the next Lucy—it's my hair, you understand—so he showed me a pratfall. That's the noise you heard, Rollie taking a pratfall down the stairs." She stopped speaking for a moment to look up at Josh. "You did it just like him, Joe. Maybe you should think about going into the movies." Then, aware she was treading on thin ice, Mandy began giggling all over again.

Josh shrugged Mandy's arm away and reached up with both hands to wipe the shaving cream from his skin. He turned to her for a second, foam-covered hands outstretched as if entertaining the idea of smearing the stuff all over her face, then dropped his hands to his sides.

"Mandy, I think I'll finish shaving now, if you don't mind. Rollie," he said with great dignity, considering he was standing in the living room looking like a clown who had run amok in a nudist camp. Then he turned to hold out one sticky hand to the waiter. "Nice meeting you. Good luck with your career."

Rollie looked down at the shaving-cream-coated hand and knew it was time to pay the piper. The guy could have me fired, he thought worriedly. Hell, the guy could punch my lights out and I wouldn't blame him. If he's willing to settle for this, who am I to complain? "Sir," Rollie gulped, sticking out his own hand bravely and taking Josh's firmly in his, feeling the cream squishing coldly between his fingers. "My pleasure entirely."

Josh took back his hand, looked down at Rollie's, now covered with shaving cream, and smiled. "Not entirely,

Rollie," he soothed, feeling slightly mollified. "Not entirely. Come back later, and we'll see if the director can find a place for you in the filming, okay?"

Rollie's jaw dropped open. "You're kidding!" he exclaimed, hardly believing his good luck. "No, you're not kidding, are you? Hey, you're all right, sir." He fairly danced his way to the door, laughing as he declined the tip Mandy was holding out for him. "I'll be back later, folks. Hey, thank you. Thank you very much!"

Once the door had closed behind the ecstatic waiter, Mandy turned to look at Josh, who was already on his way back up the stairs. "Hey, husband," she called, stopping him in his tracks.

He looked down at her, wondering if she was going to try to score another few points off his embarrassing tumble down the stairs. "Yes?" he prodded, wishing she'd get it over with quickly. He already felt lower than a snake's belly. Lord only knew there were more romantic ways of falling at a lady's feet, none of them having anything to do with shaving cream.

Mandy tipped her head to one side, her emerald eyes soft and glowing as she looked up at him. "You're all right, you know. Under those designer clothes you wear beats a heart of pure marshmallow."

Leaning on the banister, Josh let his chin drop onto his chest in relief. Relief and the sudden realization that Mandy's words had somehow made him feel that the whole incident had been worth it, just to have gained her approval.

Raising his head, he said softly, "You're okay, too, Amanda Elizabeth." As he saw her eyes beginning to get a bit misty, he added teasingly, "But you'd better not let Rollie's ideas go to your head. You're no Lucy—Ethel maybe, but no Lucy. Keep my coffee hot, will you? I'll be back down in a minute.''

After wrapping an oversize white linen napkin around the coffeepot to keep it warm, Mandy crossed the carpet to look out at the view once more. This time, in her mind's eye, she could see two horses—and two riders—chasing away the world as they galloped along beside each other through the surf. The vision made her feel good, and for now, that was enough.

Chapter Six

By midafternoon Mandy was thoroughly disenchanted with the wonderful worlds of acting and television, not that she had ever had any desire to be an actress since her disastrous debut as a cabbage in the third-grade good-health pageant.

Filming, she had discovered to her dismay, consisted more of standing around and waiting than it did of actually performing in front of the camera. For one thing, Herb and Chuck had spent nearly two hours covering the picture window with huge sheets of white paper.

They had explained that although they wanted the drapes open for the shot, the light from the sun and artificial light were two different shades—one blue, one green (Mandy hadn't been interested enough to remember which was which)—and therefore it was necessary to block the outside light.

Then, once the lighting had been set up to Chuck's satisfaction, Lois had gotten the brainstorm of moving the couch to a new location in front of the window, saying something about the oil paintings on the wall over the couch being "too busy" for the scene she had planned. That set the lighting job back a full hour, and Mandy decided to take a bubble bath to pass the time.

She really wanted to go outside and walk along the boardwalk. She wanted to run down to the beach and watch the little children play in the sand. *She* wanted to play in the sand, too, feel its cool dampness beneath her hands as she fashioned a fairy castle and then watched it disappear with the incoming tide.

Mostly, she wanted Josh to see her in her new bathing suit, a one-piece emerald-green-on-white print that Marion had said made her legs look like they went all the way up to her neck. She wanted to kneel over him as he lay on a blanket in the sun-kissed sand and slowly rub warm suntan oil onto his muscular back. She wanted—oh, Lord, she wanted so much, wanted it with every tingling cell in her body.

Definitely, she thought as she looked across the room to where Josh was sitting on the floor, deep in conversation with Herb, it's definitely more than time for a bubble bath. Maybe even a cold shower. "I'm going upstairs for a while, Lois," she informed the director, who was just then waffling about moving the couch closer to the corner and making room for a table and lamp "to make it look more homey, less staged."

"Good idea, Mandy," Lois agreed, waving her on her way without even turning around. "You need some more makeup anyway, toots. Glad you realized it."

Mandy hadn't realized anything of the kind. She thrust out her bottom lip, as if she could then look down and see the lipstick she had applied so carefully only an hour earlier. "More lipstick, you mean, right?" she asked, knowing that she had already applied more makeup that morning in anticipation of the filming than she had ever used at one time before in her life.

Lois laughed shrilly. "More *everything*, my dear, unless you want to look like a ghost on camera. And fluff up your hair, okay? It'll photograph too flat the way it is. Maybe a French twist and a sculpted top—Joe, what do you think?"

Josh took in Mandy's mulish expression and decided that discretion was the better part of valor. Besides, it wouldn't serve his purpose if Lois's ideas transformed Mandy to the point that her own grandfather wouldn't recognize her. "I think my wife looks just great as she is, Lois," he said slowly. "Besides, if you pile her hair too high on the top of her head, she'll end up looking like one of those coneheads on those old *Saturday Night Live* shows, right, darling?"

Some help he is, Mandy fumed silently, her hands closing into fists at her sides. He was probably the sort of boy scout who only helped old ladies across the street if they didn't want to go. "You mean, like you looked just like Chevy Chase this morning when you fell down the steps, dearest? Lois, did I tell you about Joe's pratfall? He was all covered in shaving cream and—"

"Okay, okay, I give up!" Josh cut in hurriedly, avoiding Mandy's triumphant grin. And the score remains tied, he thought, wincing slightly. "Do you think my wife needs more makeup, Herb?" he then asked the cameraman, believing that at the moment an outside opinion was the safest way to go.

As far as Josh was concerned, Mandy looked good enough to eat as she was, and he never was the sort who liked too much makeup on a woman in the first place. A man felt afraid to touch such perfection, let alone make love to it. Mandy looked, well—approachable. "Herb?" he pushed as the man seemed to be ignoring him to concentrate on adjusting something on his camera.

Herb finally stood up, lifted the camera to his shoulder and swung it around to capture Mandy in his sights like a marksman taking aim on some unsuspecting prey. "Looks like a beached flounder," he said baldly, switching off the camera and putting it back in its case before sitting back down beside Josh.

"Thanks, Herb," Josh said under his breath. "You've been a big help. Remind me to check with you before I go for the physical exam for the life-insurance policy I'm thinking of taking out."

"Put the makeup on until you think you should be out walking the streets, Mandy," Chuck put in encouragingly when he suspected that the young woman was about to burst into tears. "When you figure you look like a down-at-the-heels hooker, you'll have just enough on for the camera."

"What about him?" Mandy protested pettishly, as Josh laughed weakly at her predicament. "Don't men have to have makeup, too? Why's everybody picking on me?"

Lois looked at Josh assessingly, then shook her head. "He's so evenly tan he'll hardly need anything more than a light dusting of powder on his face, neck and hands. It's pale redheads like you, Mandy, who need the most help. Sorry."

Seeing Josh's smug smile, which seemed to say, "See, I told you that you were a stereotype," Mandy gave up the fight and went upstairs for her bath. In the end, Lois had to wield the makeup brush herself, as Mandy still hadn't made her cheeks pink enough to suit the director. The filming, which consisted of nothing more than a repeated panning of the room as Mandy and Josh sat on the couch holding hands and smiling like village idiots, was at last completed.

"That's it?" Mandy squeaked incredulously as the hot lights were finally turned off. "All that carrying on for five puny minutes of film? It's six o'clock, almost time for dinner, and that's all you've gotten done? I don't believe it!"

"Now, now, darling, temper, temper," Josh soothed, although he was just as angry as she was at the waste of time. But it was necessary scene setting, and would be helpful to him in the long run. "Go upstairs like a good little bride and scrub that gunk off your face so I can take you to dinner. You know how I love Italian food. I made reservations at the Il Verdi, here in the hotel."

"And I canceled them," Lois slipped in firmly as she helped Chuck rewrap some of the seeming miles of electrical cord that were needed for the equipment. "We're going to film you eating hot dogs on the boardwalk, folks, so Mandy, keep your makeup on and just go grab a sweater in case it gets chilly. It will probably be pretty late before we can wrap up filming for the day."

"Joe?" Mandy begged weakly, looking at him with mute appeal in her eyes. If it took as long to set up shots outdoors as it did in the hotel room, they wouldn't get to eat until midnight. Besides, nobody could possibly love Italian food more than she did. "Do we have to?"

The phone in the suite rang then, causing Lois to say that it must be her station calling her about something important. "I left this number at the desk," she explained with that air of self-importance that was beginning to grate on Mandy's nerves, before removing one large pink pearl earring and picking up the phone.

But the call was for "Joe Tremaine." "Run along up-stairs, darling, and grab a sweater," he called as he went to answer the phone. "We have to eat anyway, so we might as well be good little soldiers. Maybe Lois will promise us a free morning tomorrow if we behave to-night. Isn't that right, Lois?" There was a hint of steel in his voice that sounded more like it belonged in a board-room than on a boardwalk, and Chuck took a moment from his chores to glance sharply at the happy bride-groom.

The director, who wouldn't have noticed Josh's change of tone even if she'd been intelligent enough to interpret it, selfishly considered his suggestion. Hoping she had been correctly reading the signals Chuck had been send-ing her all day, she quickly agreed to the compromise. Who knew what the night might bring if she played her cards right. Maybe a late start tomorrow morning would work well for everyone.

"Oh, all right," Mandy gave in grudgingly. "I'll only be a minute." She went part of the way up the stairs be-fore she heard her "husband" say into the phone, "Joe Tremaine here," and was struck by a sudden curiosity as to the identity of Joe's caller. Racing up the rest of the steps, she threw herself down on the large bed, took a deep breath, and carefully lifted the receiver of the bed-side phone.

"So, *Joe*, how's it going?" she heard a deep, skeptical voice ask. She had been right in thinking that Joe hadn't been using his real first name, she told herself, feeling satisfied to know that her instincts had proven correct. She had noticed that he had never answered immedi-ately whenever she called him by name. This must be his superior on the phone, calling for an update on the in-vestigation of Herb the cameraman.

"The weather's quite warm here, Dad, and I believe it may even get hotter." Mandy made a face at the receiver. "Dad!" she mouthed silently. Couldn't he be any more inventive than that? What a ridiculous code name for an investigator.

"How much longer do you intend to be gone?" the man called Dad asked. "One of the guys here, some smooth operator named Vic Harrison, has been asking some pretty probing questions around the studio. As a matter of fact, I think I just might have a few rather probing questions of my own for you, *Mr. Tremaine.*"

"Give me a couple more days, Dad, then I'll have everything I need to take care of that little business we talked about in your office the other night, okay? Just cut me some slack. If there's no emergency, you shouldn't have called." Josh's voice was barely above a whisper, as if he was trying not to let anyone else in the room downstairs overhear what he was saying into the phone. "Give my best to Mom, will you," he then said in a much louder voice. "Thanks so much for calling. Bye now."

"Don't you hang up on me, you scoundrel!" the other voice yelled into the phone, hurting Mandy's ear. She could hear the click of the living-room phone as Joe hung up downstairs. "What was that clicking noise? Are you still there?" the exasperated voice continued, for as long as Mandy was listening, the line would remain open. "Josh? Answer me, damn it! Josh!"

Mandy set the phone down quietly and silently repeated the name she had overheard. Josh. Joshua? A slight smile formed on her face as she realized she had just had her first success as an investigator, even if it had nothing to do with Herb. "Josh," she breathed softly before she rolled over and stood up, heading for the closet to search out her navy sweater. "I like it."

The beach lay deserted below them as they looked out toward the night-darkened sea. The filming had finally been completed two hours earlier, after Mandy had declared she couldn't bite into another hot dog even if someone held a loaded gun to her head.

Lois had reshot the scene at the hot-dog stand twelve times, each take requiring fresh hot dogs for both Josh and Mandy. If a passerby hadn't stopped to make a victory sign with his fingers into the camera, then the hot-dog man, whom Josh had secretly thought was overplaying his part, had dropped the hot dog he was trying to flip into the roll without ever once taking his eyes off the camera.

And when neither of those two things had happened, either Mandy's hot dog had been so hot it burned her mouth, causing her to screech and spit it out, or Josh had dribbled mustard onto the front of his shirt—anything to have Lois yell, "Cut," yet again. The one time everything had gone as planned, Herb realized he had forgotten to change the tape in the camera. All in all, it wasn't a memorable two hours for any of them—excepting maybe the camera-hungry hot-dog man.

Even the footage of the two happy newlyweds strolling down the boardwalk gazing soulfully into each other's eyes as they wound their way through the throng of late-day bathers and aspiring slot-machine millionaires had required an hour of setup time and seven takes.

Chuck's explanation about getting the natural light and the darkness to play together without making too many shadows had gone completely over Mandy's head, and she had felt no need to wave the information goodbye as it had flown past.

But finally the filming was over, and the crew had all gone back to the Tropicana, Lois helpfully toting a good bit of Chuck's gear for him while Herb, his usual taciturn self, mumbled something about hitting the casino for a while before calling it a night.

Josh had waved them on their way, then, taking Mandy's arm, had purposefully begun walking along the boardwalk in the opposite direction. "I thought they'd never leave," he had said, grinning down at her before sliding his arm across her shoulders and pulling her against him as they walked along.

"Amen," Mandy agreed with a sigh, laying her cheek against his arm. She felt more comfortable with him at that moment than she had since they had met. She felt like they were coconspirators, playing hooky from school. "Where are we going?" she asked, looking around at the people who all seemed to be rushing somewhere. "Not that I care, you understand, as long as we don't have to drag a film crew with us."

"That's only natural, oh wife of mine. You shouldn't care where we're going, as long as we're together."

Mandy raised her head to look up at his chiseled chin. "Oh, brother, spare me the dramatics! The camera's off, Mr. Tremaine. You can stop pretending now, or is this what they call method acting?"

He looked down at her, his warm breath fanning her cheek. "You want to go back to the hotel? Never let it be said I'm not the agreeable sort."

Mandy closed her eyes a second, savoring his closeness. "No," she answered, deciding it was time she indulged herself a little, and hang the consequences. "I want to walk along the boardwalk with you, oh husband of mine," she paraphrased lightly, hoping he wouldn't pull away from her.

And walk they did, up and down the crowded boardwalk, admiring the brightly lit casinos and making up little stories about some of the more interesting-looking people they passed along the way.

"See that tall lady over there talking to the policeman?" Josh had pointed out as they walked along. "She's really Sergeant Stanley Kopchek, from the city vice detail."

"Do tell?" Mandy commented, going along with the game. "Please, Inspector, won't you give me the benefit of all your years of police work? Exactly what is it that gives him away?"

"It's elementary, my dear. The man walks like a duck. *All* policemen walk like ducks."

Mandy sniffed in disbelief. "You're reaching, Joe. That's no clue. You should see my great-aunt Alice. When we visited her when I was a kid I always held my breath, waiting for her to quack."

"Okay," he admitted, shrugging. "Maybe it's his five o'clock shadow that tipped me off."

"That, and his sideburns, right?" Mandy said, giving him a playful jab in the ribs. Then, looking around, she spied another likely subject. "Catch that one over by the railing, the guy in the plaid sport coat. What does he do for a living, oh wise one?"

Josh measured the man with a glance, taking in the bright orange-and-green plaid coat, the orange slacks and the wing-tip shoes. "You're making this too easy. Our plaid man's name is Thaddeus W. McGee, Esquire, and he's a vacationing mortician from the Midwest," he pronounced at last, sending Mandy into a fit of giggles.

They had stopped several times to look into shop windows, selecting outlandish presents for everyone they knew. At a small stand that was just closing for the night Mandy started jumping up and down, tugging at his arm and pleading until Josh stopped and bought her some chocolate marshmallow fudge and picked out some fresh peanut brittle for himself.

They halted again in front of a saltwater-taffy shop, where Mandy stood enthralled as the huge metal arms of the taffy-pulling machine twisted the candy into long, shining strands. Josh threatened to remove her bodily but she refused to budge until he had bought her three large boxes of the sugary confection to take back for the children at the nursery school.

At last, long past midnight, they walked across the width of the boardwalk to stand at the railing along a deserted stretch of the beach to share a quiet moment looking out over the ocean. They were silent for some minutes, but it was a shared silence that brought a measure of peace to both of them.

"What are you thinking?" Josh asked quietly at last, wondering why he was breaking the mood.

Mandy had been thinking about telling him that she had discovered his real name—or at least part of it. Not wanting him to know what she had learned until she felt sure of his reaction, she countered with a question of her own. "What have you found out so far about Herb? The two of you were talking together a lot this morning back at the hotel. He seems rather closemouthed, doesn't he? And he hasn't made a single pass at me, either, so I guess he doesn't go after married women."

So we're back to that, are we, Josh thought unhappily. This pretense of investigating Herb was beginning to wear on him. Maybe if the guy was even the least bit interesting it wouldn't be so bad. But Herb the cameraman was just about the most boring, one-dimensional individual Josh had ever met. "I think I'm on to something, Mandy," he lied smoothly, "but Herb's only small potatoes. I'll have to get back to Allentown before I can learn anything else.''

There, he thought smugly, that ought to put an end to this Herb nonsense. The guy was beginning to get in the way of his real reason for agreeing to do the damned filming in the first place. Why, he asked himself, as he realized that the thought of his plans for the film made him feel like a first-class rat, am I thinking about that business now?

"Does that mean you're going to leave tomorrow?"

Josh could hear the dismay in Mandy's voice and mentally kicked himself for enjoying it. "You aren't going to get rid of me that easily, wife. No, I haven't had a vacation in a long time, Mandy," he assured her. "I can't see any reason not to stick around and see this thing through. Don't worry, the kids' stereo is safe.''

Mandy blinked twice at Josh's words. The stereo. Good grief, she had forgotten all about it! To cover her lapse, she asked quickly, "If Herb's a dead end, who do you go after next? I mean, the big boss must be in Allentown, right?" Her voice lowered to a conspiratorial whisper. "Do you think Vic Harrison is involved, now that you've talked with Herb? I know you denied it before, but then when I heard—''

She was off again, Josh thought, hiding a smile, fashioning yet another melodrama in that fertile imagination of hers. Suddenly he realized that Mandy had stopped talking, cutting off her words in mid-fantasy. "Mandy?" he prodded, noticing her tightly closed lips. "Oh, so that's it, isn't it? You were eavesdropping from the bedroom earlier when I talked to my—''

"Dad?" she said on a sneer. "Really, Joe, surely you could have worked out a better code name than that. I mean, really!''

Josh raised his eyebrows and stared at her, hardly believing his luck. Bless her beautiful, twisted logic, which kept her from seeing what was staring her right in the eyes. "We can't all be double-o-sevens, you know. And don't change the subject. What were you doing snooping in on my telephone conversation? That's dirty pool, lady."

Mandy was feeling just guilty enough about learning his real name—even if he didn't know she had—to take his criticism without hitting back. "What do you think Lois has planned for tomorrow, Joe?" she asked, turning back to face the ocean, letting him know that he'd get no apology from her, even if he deserved one. "She said something about setting up a dancing sequence in the suite's living room because it would be easier to light it there, but I can't figure out how we're supposed to dance on carpeting. I mean, you really can't—"

Her swift flow of words was cut off by the sound of Josh's laughter. "God, how I love it when you go off on a tangent. What do you do—about six hundred words a minute? Doesn't your tongue ever get chapped by the breeze?"

Closing her mouth with a decided snap, Mandy whirled on her heels and made to walk away from the railing, but Josh was too quick for her. "Hold it, wife, where do you think you're going?"

"I'm going to look for Sergeant Stanley Kopchek, who else?" she said between clenched teeth. "Maybe if I ask him nicely he'll arrest you for being a public nuisance." She looked down at the hand that held her arm, then glared up into his face. "Let go of my arm, buster, before I show you what I learned in lesson two of that self-defense show. Believe me, it isn't pretty."

"I can't believe you'd ever hurt anyone on purpose," Josh observed, suddenly serious. "You don't have an evil bone in your body. I'll bet you even have a hard time killing bugs."

"Spiders," she answered weakly, mesmerized by his warm, intense expression.

"What?" he asked automatically, wondering how anyone could possibly have such vivid green eyes. He could see their color even in this dim half-light.

"I said spiders. They're the worst, you know, what with all those hairy legs. I can't kill them at all, but not because I don't want to hurt them. They scare me. I always have to call Mrs. Thorton from downstairs to kill them, but she takes such delight in it that mostly I just pray they'll find a crack in the wall and go away."

"I know I warned you not to start liking me too much, but you don't play fair, lady, not warning me in return," Josh confessed quietly, gathering her into his arms and pulling her back against the railing. "I think I'm beginning to fall in love with you, Amanda Elizabeth Tremaine. What do you think of that?"

"I—I don't know what to think," Mandy told him honestly, melting against his lean, hard frame. "You—you don't really know anything about me. And, well, you can hardly say I know anything about you." Oh Lord, but his arms felt good around her. "I mean, it could just be proximity—isn't that what they say happens when two people spend all their time together and begin thinking that they feel something for each other that they wouldn't feel if they weren't in such close proximity?"

"Do they really say all that?" Josh asked in amused fascination, leaning down to nibble on her earlobe.

"Yes, yes they do," she rushed on, trying to fill the night with anything but the echo of his startling confession. "And it is true that we hardly know one another, you know it is. I *like* you, honestly I do." She closed her eyes with a sigh. "Very much. But I don't even know where you live, or what you really do. And you don't know much more about me. I wasn't born a nursery-school teacher, you know. I have lived for nearly a full quarter century."

"When you say it that way you sound older than me, and I'm thirty-two." He slid his mouth down the side of her throat, causing an involuntary moan to slide past her lips. All his plans for revenge against her grandfather, all his long-held beliefs that love 'em and leave 'em should have been his family motto, fled his mind without regret. "You know that I'm not a serial killer and I know that you're a delightful innocent who loves bubble baths and sugary candy. What else is there to know?"

He could feel her stiffening in his arms before she actually pulled away, walking to a spot farther down the railing, her arms wrapped around her upper body. "What's the matter?" he asked tightly, putting a hand on her arm. "Somehow I get the feeling I just pushed the wrong button."

When Mandy turned around, tears were standing in the corners of her eyes, ready to spill over if she so much as blinked. "I—I'm very flattered that you think you're falling in love with me, Joe, but until we can be completely honest with each other, I think it's best if we continue on as we were." Her voice might have been trembling, but her chin was firm, determined.

She called him Joe, Josh told himself, hiding the pain that direct jab at his conscience provoked. Mandy was right, he was going too fast. It must be the moonlight, he lied inwardly, knowing he was only kidding himself, just as he had been kidding himself ever since he had impulsively taken Mandy's part at WFML that first day.

Why did she have to be Mandy *Tremaine*? Why had he been so damned smart as to connect her with Alexander Tremaine? Why did he ever hatch this stupid plan for revenge in the first place? And what was Mandy hiding? It wasn't just *his* past that concerned her; of that he was sure. Maybe she was just as disenchanted with her grandfather as he was—after all, she had run away from their home more than three years ago without leaving a trace. It had been the talk of the town for a while, Mandy's disappearance. That, and the incident with Dave Benjamin that had occurred the same week.

Why didn't he say something? Mandy felt she was going to scream if he didn't soon say something, do something. Josh was just staring out at the ocean, still holding tight to one of her arms. "Joe?" He was so deep in his own thoughts that he didn't hear her. "Joe? Are you angry with me? Please don't be angry with me."

Something in the pleading tone of her voice got through to him, and he shook his head, looking away from the dark ocean and straight into her eyes. "You're a tough cookie, Amanda Elizabeth," he confided softly. "But you're right. I think it's time we called it a night. Truce?" he offered, as she had the day before in the limousine.

And, as he had done the day before, she smiled wickedly and scoffed, "Truce? Oh, no. Not by the hair of my chinny-chin-chin!"

Mandy lay in the middle of the huge bed as moonlight streamed in through the large picture windows, casting strange, moving patterns on the tangled sheets. She had been in bed for almost an hour, but she was no nearer to finding the sleep she craved than she had been when she first laid her head on the pillow.

"I think I'm falling in love with you," Josh had said, and she could still hear his low, husky voice repeating the words over and over inside her head. She closed her eyes tightly, as if in pain. The man tells me he thinks he's falling in love with me, she thought, and what do I do?

I open my big mouth and make a complete fool of myself, *that's* what I do! she lamented, mentally answering her own question, before rolling over to hide her burning cheeks in the pillow. Then I do the worst, the very worst thing of all, she thought, shuddering. I tell him I *like* him! God! He must have been holding his breath, thinking that at any minute I'd ask him to exchange friendship rings!

She flopped over onto her back to stare at the ceiling. Everything was moving so fast—too fast—and Mandy was having difficulty catching her breath. After all, as she had told herself all during the long, silent walk back to the Tropicana, they had known each other less than a week. Love didn't grow in such a short time, did it? Especially love between two people who really knew less than nothing about each other?

And if he did know everything about me, about Grandfather? she dared to ask herself, feeling it was safe to think about the subject as she lay in the dark, alone. And what about Dave? What would Josh say if he knew about my involvement with Dave? Would he still think he loved me then? A tear rolled down her cheek, to lose itself in the pillowcase. Would Josh still love me like I love him? Because I do love him, very, very much. Would he be happy that I loved him, or would he run from me as fast as his legs could carry him? Oh, why does everything have to be so complicated?

While Mandy wrestled with her demons in the dark bedroom at the top of the spiral staircase, Josh lay on the pulled-out couch in the living room, trying to decide what he should do next. "Making a clean breast of things might not be such a bad idea, Phillips," he mused aloud, chuckling quietly as he told himself he had definitely picked up Mandy's habit of talking to herself.

Shrugging as he realized that talking to himself was the least of his problems, he decided he might as well go with the flow, and see where it led him. "Okay, Phillips, old boy, start talking. Let's see. First I'd say, 'Mandy, I have something to tell you. My name isn't Joe. It's Josh, Joshua Phillips, actually.'"

He shook his head slightly. "That wouldn't surprise her. She's been smelling a rat all along about my phony investigator story. No, it's the next step that might upset her, the part where I tell her I'm from Southampton, just like she is. Since we've only lived there for the past five years, and she was away at that college in Switzerland, or just plain missing, for most of that time, that little piece of information will come as something of a surprise.

"Then what, Phillips? If she hasn't either fainted or run away, figuring that you knew who she was all along, you'd still have to tell her about the plot to revenge yourself on old Matthew Tremaine for what he did to Dave Benjamin. How you were going to send him the videotape of you and his missing granddaughter cavorting in sin in Atlantic City, just so he could sit up there in his castle overlooking the beach and turn purple with rage. How were you planning to drop that little bomb and still convince her you love her?"

Josh rolled onto his side and gave his pillow half a dozen solid whacks with his fist. "Mandy might be an idealistic, naive little angel, Phillips, but if she doesn't haul off and belt you on the spot you don't know your sweet Carrot Top half as well as you think you do."

So saying, Josh got up to turn on the light and look at the television listings, hoping there was a late-night movie on that would be bad enough to punish him for his sins.

Chapter Seven

No, no, *no*! Mandy, you're still doing it all wrong. You're too tense." Lois Lamour waved her hands in barely controlled anger, signaling Herb to turn off the camera. Walking over to sit down on the corner of the large bed, the director said tightly, "Mandy, you are enjoying a lovely breakfast in bed with your handsome, brand-new husband. You are not, not—" Suddenly Lois was at a loss for words.

"You're not eating your last meal of stale bread and ditch water before facing the firing squad," Chuck put in neatly, taking up the slack when Lois's try at creativity failed to come up with a reasonable comparison.

"Thank you, Chuck," Lois intoned coldly, throwing the technician a dirty look before redirecting her attention to Mandy. "Okay, people, let's try it again. Now, Mandy, please, loosen up! We still have that casino footage to get in today."

Mandy closed her eyes and counted to ten, trying to keep herself from picking up the juicy grapefruit half that lay in front of her on the breakfast tray and grinding it into Lois Lamour's smirking face. "I'm really sorry, Lois," she said instead, swallowing down hard on her anger. "It's just—it's just so *staged*. I mean, whoever heard of a couple having breakfast in bed while a waiter hovers over them?"

"Hey, I'm playing my role right!" Rollie protested, straightening his bow tie as he stood beside the bed, coffeepot at the ready. "Besides, Mr. Tremaine here promised me this part. Tell her, Mr. Tremaine. This is my chance at the big time."

"Yes, darling," Josh said, reaching a hand over to pat Mandy's stiff shoulder as he sat close beside her in the middle of the bed. "Rollie's giving the performance of his career. But you've got to smile up at him when he pours you another cup of coffee, not cringe down under the sheets as if he were offering you decaffeinated hemlock."

Shooting her bed companion a look that should have had him pulling the covers over his own head for protection, Mandy apologized to Rollie, assuring him that she would try to do better on the next take. "But I still don't see why we can't have the breakfast scene at the table in front of the window. I mean, I know Miss America is photographed every year having breakfast in bed after winning the pageant, but she's wearing a crown and holding a bouquet of roses—not sitting beside a man who's wearing a pair of silk pajamas and a satisfied grin. Besides, Lois, showing newlyweds having breakfast in bed is so trite, don't you think?"

Obviously Lois didn't so think, and hadn't throughout the long hour Mandy had fought the plan to show the pajama-clad pair happily propped up against their pillows sharing an intimate morning-after catered breakfast.

"Have to redo the lighting for that," Herb put in shortly, once more lifting the mobile camera to his shoulder and squinting at Mandy through the lens.

"Thank you for that absolutely *scintillating* little piece of information, Herb," Mandy bit out testily before pulling a face for the cameraman. "*Yikes!* You cut that out!"

Josh withdrew his hand—the one that had just slipped under the covers to reach over and tickle her rib cage. "Cut what out?" he asked innocently. His fingertips tingled from their brief contact with Mandy's soft, silk-covered skin. As far as he was concerned, this was Lois's best idea yet, and he had been thoroughly enjoying himself all morning. "Lois?" he inquired now, looking across the bed at the director. "If Mandy and I could have a few moments alone, I think I can find a way to convince her to behave."

Chuck was the first to rise, switching off his playback machine and heading for the staircase that led to the living room. "Come on, Lois," he called back over his shoulder. "Can't you take a hint? They want to be alone for a couple of minutes. Rollie? Herb?"

Rollie followed. Herb was right behind him, remembering that there were still two fresh prune Danish pastries on the coffee tray in the living room, and Lois was left with no choice but to agree. "Just don't muss her makeup," she warned by way of a parting shot before joining the rest of the film crew downstairs.

"Don't muss her makeup, don't muss her makeup," Mandy parroted shrilly, waggling her head back and forth. "I could learn to hate that broad," she said nastily once the crew had disappeared.

"Alone at last," Josh growled playfully, leering over at Mandy menacingly after lifting the lap trays and moving them to the bottom of the bed. "Now, wife, what seems to be the problem?"

Mandy looked at him. He appeared more handsome than he had a right to in his burgundy pajamas. She exploded, even if she held her voice down to a fierce whisper. "I'm sitting in bed in my nightgown, beside a man dressed in silk pajamas—a man who, by the way, is *not* my husband—while Rollie Estrada skips around the bed spouting bad Shakespeare and Lois and the rest of them throw me directions that make me feel like I've landed in the middle of an R-rated movie, and *you* ask me what's the matter? Why, Joe, I'm surprised at you. How could you possibly not guess why I'm upset? I'm simply devastated because I just broke a nail—any fool would know that!"

"I thought you said you were a morning person," Josh said brightly, trying to hold back his amusement. "Maybe if you had another cup of coffee—"

"You make me drink one more cup of coffee and I'm going to start screaming," Mandy shot back tightly. "And you're the worst of all, as if you didn't know it already. 'Certainly, Lois'…'I think that's a marvelous idea, Lois'…'Let me kiss your skinny feet, Lois.' Do you have to agree with everything that idiot woman says? Kisses over coffee. Good Lord, I thought I was going to throw up!"

"It's part of the deal, Mandy," he reminded her, running his hand slowly along one of her peignoir's white silken sleeves. "Remember all those dear little kiddies back at the nursery school who are depending on you to keep their new stereo safe? Come on, champ, do it for the Gipper!''

Mandy thought about it for a few moments, then wiggled around under the covers to face her tormentor. ''Only if you promise to stop doing things to me under the covers.''

''Doing things?'' Josh pretended to be horrified. ''Whatever do you mean?''

''I mean I nearly choked on my scrambled eggs when you started running your toes up and down my leg. I thought Lois was going to have a spasm.''

''You're overreacting, Mandy, Lois didn't notice anything. Besides, I kinda liked it, myself.''

Mandy's lips curled derisively. ''You would. Now—do you promise?'' Deep inside her, Mandy was thanking Josh for allowing them to slip back into their accustomed roles so easily this morning—sniping at each other and generally keeping things light.

The scene in the bed would have been intolerable otherwise, considering the fact that having his body pressed so closely against hers was conjuring up some very unnursery-school-teacher fantasies that had her following her heart and blurting out that she had fallen madly, hopelessly in love with a near stranger.

Josh watched the play of emotions on Mandy's expressive face. It had taken every ounce of self-control he'd had to keep himself from climbing those stairs last night and taking what he was sure she would have been willing to give. But logic—and three very bad movies—had won out in the end, and he was determined this morning to go slowly, waiting until she was ready before making his move—before telling her the whole truth and begging her to love him anyway.

"Well? Do you promise? Or have you finally realized that I'm right, and you're going downstairs to tell Lois that she and her stupid ideas can go take a hike? Anyone would think she's after an Emmy for this program."

Josh looked at Mandy's flushed cheeks and sparkling green eyes. "And Rollie's looking for an Academy Award," he added, a smile hovering on his lips. "It would be heartless to disappoint them, wouldn't it? Okay, I'll behave, if *you* promise to do your part so that we can be done with this and get dressed. I don't like the way Lois has been looking at me. Chuck told me he nearly had to beat her away with a stick last night, and I don't like the idea of parading in my pajamas in front of lovesick females on the rebound."

"You're a recently married man, Joe, Lois wouldn't go after you," Mandy reminded him, motioning for him to replace her lap tray across her knees. "But I have intercepted a couple of the looks she's been throwing Rollie's way. How desperate do you think our waiter is to get into television?"

Josh settled his own lap tray over his knees before turning to wink at Mandy. "*Nobody's* that desperate, darling. Now, what do you say we get this show on the road? Gimme a kiss for good luck."

Mandy pulled back slightly, finally relaxing enough to joke with him. "As long as you promise not to muss my makeup."

"We have one thousand four hundred and seventy-one slot machines here in Slot City, ranging from the nickel slots to our mini-Berthas. It's so big, in fact, that we here at the Tropicana elected a mayor of Slot City, though he's really more of an ambassador of goodwill. That's him over there—the one in the sequined tuxedo and top hat."

The attractive young woman, one of the casino hotel's publicity managers, was conducting a guided tour for the newlyweds and the film crew, explaining some of the finer points of the area they were walking through.

"Look, Joe," Mandy said, reading the pamphlet she had picked up on her way into the casino. "It says here that Slot City is so big it's actually divided into streets. There's Million Dollar Drive and Big Bertha Boulevard, even a Jackpot Lane. I can't believe it!"

Josh looked down at Mandy's smiling face, feeling partly responsible for the glow she had been wearing ever since the very tender, extremely satisfying kiss they had shared earlier over the breakfast trays before he had called Lois back upstairs to continue the filming. It had been he who had pulled away from their embrace first, although it had taken every iota of willpower he possessed to do it, leaving Mandy still leaning toward him, her eyes closed and a dreamy smile on her lips.

The scene had then been completed without a hitch, and after firmly declining Chuck's offer to join the three crew members for lunch at the Back Stage Deli, he and Mandy had taken turns getting dressed in the bathroom before allowing the grateful Rollie to make good his promise to treat them to hamburgers at the Brasserie. The waiter's inane chatter had carried them neatly through lunch, and Josh actually found himself looking forward to the filming inside the casino.

He took the brochure from her hand, paging through it idly to look at the full-color pictures of the many streets in the multilevel Slot City, all of them seeming to have their own particular theme. "It says here that there's a fruit market somewhere near Jackpot Lane, with chandeliers made up like bunches of cherries, plums, oranges and—"

"Watermelons!" Mandy exclaimed, laughing delight-edly as she leaned against his side and read the pamphlet with him. "This I have got to see. There's nothing better in the world than our great American tendency to take things to extremes. Watermelon chandeliers and slot machines, what a combination."

Lois soon agreed that the fruit market seemed an ideal location for the scene she had planned, and soon Josh and Mandy were standing side by side in front of two slot machines, large cups full of quarters at the ready. "Careful you don't get tennis elbow from pulling on that handle," Josh whispered as Chuck tried to discourage passersby from horning in on the shot Herb was about to film.

"This is silly," Mandy complained, dropping quarter after quarter in the slot and watching the pictures of fruit spinning around dizzily before coming to a halt. "Feed in a quarter, pull down on the handle, watch the little windows mixing up a fruit salad, and then wave your quarter goodbye forever. I can't see how people can honestly say they enjoy this."

"According to the publicity manager, some guy en-joyed himself to the tune of over two million dollars, all won on Million Dollar Drive somewhere here in Slot City. I can't say for sure that it would make all this seem worthwhile to you, but it sure as hell works for me."

Mandy turned to Josh in amazement. "Two—two *million* dollars?" she asked, gasping for breath. "Play-ing a slot machine? That's almost obscene!"

"Yeah," Josh agreed, feeding in five quarters at one time as Herb kept the camera rolling. "All that scream-ing, all those lights blinking and sirens sounding while the mayor runs up to you in his sequined tuxedo and com-plete strangers hug and kiss you and you get your picture taken for all the newspapers. What a distasteful display. But I imagine it has its up side, too—I mean, think about it—the guy probably got himself his own personal IRS agent.''

Pulling a face at him, Mandy said scornfully, ''I'm not saying I'd turn down two million dollars, for goodness' sake. I'm not that crazy. But not too many people win that kind of money. Why, I'll bet people lose—what's that?''

A ringing sound caught her attention and a yellow light on top of her machine began blinking as it registered a win. Then she heard the clinking of quarters as the metal tray located at the bottom of the machine began filling with coins. ''Oh, my God,'' she shrieked excitedly, looking down at the cup, ''I won! Look, darling, I won! Isn't it wonderful?''

As she spoke she was scooping the small supply of quarters into her cup, her fingers trembling with excitement. ''Oh, darn, I forgot to count them. I wonder how much I won.''

''Not as much as you could have if you'd been playing more than a quarter at a time like I am,'' he told her, amused by her antics, but it was clear that she wasn't listening. She was busily feeding another quarter into the machine.

''Shh, not now. I'm on a roll, I can feel it.'' Leaning down, all the better to monitor the progress of the spinning fruit, she coaxed softly, ''Come on you pretty little watermelons, do your thing. Mandy needs a new pair of shoes.''

''That's 'baby needs a new pair of shoes,' and people say that when they shoot dice,'' Josh corrected, shaking his head as Mandy showed all the signs of going off on another of her tangents.

"Whatever. You're just jealous," she replied scornfully, "because you haven't won yet. Just don't think I'm going to share my quarters with you, because I'm not going to, so you'd better get busy and win some of your own." She grinned at him playfully, then slipped five quarters into her machine.

"I thought you said gambling was boring, a pastime for fools, and you wouldn't do it on a bet," Josh teased, then added, "hey, I think I just made a joke."

"Ha, ha," she scoffed. "I didn't think you were the type to go around saying, 'I told you so,' *husband*. It just goes to show how wrong you can be about a person. Hey! Look at that, I won again. Oh, dear, do you think I'll need another cup?"

Mandy and Josh played the slot machines in the Fruit Market until Lois at last thought they had gotten enough good film to call a halt. "Mandy," Josh urged, when she didn't seem to hear Lois's okay to stop the action, "you can stop pretending you're enjoying yourself now, the camera's off. Mandy. Mandy?"

But Mandy wasn't listening, or if she was, she wasn't heeding. Her entire being was concentrating on feeding quarters into the machine, hoping to cash in on a big one. She had won again since that first small cascade of quarters had landed in the tray, but she had lost, too, and was just about breaking even at the moment. If she just held on, just played a few more quarters into the machine, she was sure to see those lovely watermelons line up beside each other again, she just knew it.

"Looks like she's hooked," Chuck offered, reaching around Josh to disconnect one of the backlights he had set up for the scene. "Whatever you do, don't let her near the Berthas or you'll never get her out of here until she's used up every last nickel in your pocket."

Josh thanked the technician for his warning, then waved him on his way before turning back to take hold of Mandy's arm just as she was about to drop another load of quarters into the slot. "We have time for a few sets of tennis on one of the rooftop courts before dinner," he suggested, since tennis had been one of the half dozen alternate activities Mandy had suggested to Lois as being more suitable for newlywed couples to be shown enjoying than gambling in the casino.

"Tennis?" Mandy said, wrinkling up her nose in distaste. "How did you ever come up with a crazy idea like that? Who wants to go running around in this heat chasing a fuzzy ball? I want to stay here in the casino. After all, we haven't even seen most of it."

"You want to walk around for a while, is that what you're saying?" he asked her skeptically. "You realize, of course, that first you'll have to sever that umbilical cord you seem to have attached to this slot machine."

Mandy drew herself up to her full height and stared at him in exasperation. "There are over fourteen hundred slot machines in Slot City. I'll just try a few of them as we walk along. Besides, I'm beginning to think this one hates me."

Picking up both of their cups, Josh nodded his head encouragingly in the direction of nearby Jackpot Lane, and then they were off, leisurely exploring each new road and boulevard they discovered in the small town-sized casino.

They dutifully followed the row of flashing one-dollar tokens that decorated the ceiling at the corners of Million Dollar Drive and Big Bertha Boulevard, leading them down into the Slot Market to a spot where an imaginative ticker-tape reader board was set up to keep visitors up to date on all the latest Slot City news.

There wasn't an avenue they didn't walk through, re-marking on the unique lighting fixtures that were de-signed to resemble overflowing flowerpots, and playing their private game that matched outlandish occupations to many of the unsuspecting casino patrons they passed along the way.

Mandy played the slot machines at random as they walked along, laughing at the comical graphics that took the place of whirling fruit on the "knockout jackpot" machines in Cherry Court, and making jokes about playing the "lazy man's slots" as she fed quarters into the automated machines that had no pull handles to test her strength.

"They make losing your money too easy," she de-cided after putting a few dollars into a video poker ma-chine in Tropicana Gardens, where the machines nestled among the walkways and fluorescent blue flowers edged the ceiling of the room. "I think I miss my watermel-ons."

"I'll buy you a truckload for your birthday," Josh promised solemnly before taking her elbow and guiding her quickly past the busy Baccarat Pit and into the The-ater District, where the flashing neon lights and mirrors combined to recreate the glamour and excitement of Broadway.

Finally, just when Josh thought he was going to be lost forever on the streets of Slot City, they ascended to the huge Flight Deck, where dozens of different-sized bal-loons, dazzling, glowing bulbs, painted rainbows and whimsical clouds—and the ever-present slot machines—filled the soaring atrium with light and color.

"Had enough, Miss High Roller, or do you want me to buy you a green visor so you can try your luck at the blackjack tables in the main casino?" he asked, crossing his fingers behind his back as he made a silent wish they could retire to one of the darkened lounges and sip on a tall, iced drink.

Mandy was quietly taking the final tally of her cupful of quarters. "I started out in the Fruit Market with ten dollars, and I ended up here with thirteen. I played all afternoon, got to see the sights and won three whole dollars! I never thought I could have so much fun gambling." She looked up, belatedly taking in her current surroundings. "Oh, look, Joe, I think that's a real hot-air balloon over there. Isn't that clever! How do you suppose they ever got that in here?"

"They didn't," he drawled lazily, slipping his arm around her waist. "They built the casino around it."

Mandy looked at Josh consideringly. "You've had enough, haven't you, Joe? Why didn't you stop me?"

He pulled her even closer to give her a quick hug. "I've had a great time watching you have a great time, my love, that's why. I wouldn't have missed it for the world. Happy?"

"Very happy," she breathed, fascinated with the way Josh's tanned skin crinkled so sexily at the corners of his eyes when he smiled. "I honestly can't remember the last time I had this much fun, unless it was last year at the Great Allentown Fair. I won the cutest stuffed unicorn at one of the stands."

"I thought you said you didn't gamble," Josh slid in smoothly, taking the cup from her hand and adding its contents to his own, filling the cup nearly to the top.

"Not for money, that's what I meant. After all, you can hardly count unicorns, can you?"

Josh just shook his head, totally defeated by Mandy's particular brand of logic. "I can't believe you've lived so close to Atlantic City and not come here—to swim and walk on the boardwalk, I mean. I've heard the advertisements on WFML for the buses that run from Allentown to the casinos every day."

"You know, I've hardly been anywhere in years," she mused, almost to herself. Then, as she saw the question coming into his eyes, she rushed on, "I mean, I've been so busy at the nursery school, you understand, that—"

"That even a pretend honeymoon with a make-believe husband, all put to music with a hovering film crew and a secret investigation, is to be considered a treat," he ended, slowly losing his smile.

He wasn't ready to hear why she was living in such straitened circumstances in Allentown when she could be riding high on the hog in Southampton with Alexander Tremaine. He'd rather concentrate on the Mandy Tremaine who lived in a third-floor walk-up apartment and taught nursery school. "And even these last few days haven't exactly been relaxing, have they? I mean, what with me alternately sniping at you and—"

"And telling me you think you're falling in love with me?" Mandy ended huskily, putting up her fingers to press them lightly against his mouth, cutting off his words. They stood close together in the middle of the wide balcony as hopeful gamblers and casino personnel detoured around them unnoticed. "I can't think of any place I'd rather be, or anyone else I'd rather have here with me."

Josh produced a weak, lopsided smile. "Honest Injun?"

"Honest Injun—*Josh*." Her emerald eyes were opened wide as they searched for his reaction.

His head was bent down so closely to hers that he thought he could count every cherished freckle on her pert little nose. "You know who I am?" he asked, his arms tightening about her waist.

"I know *half* of who you are," she corrected, tilting her head slightly to one side. "After you hung up the phone yesterday afternoon the man you called Dad said your name—he yelled it, actually. I don't think he's too overjoyed with you right now, Josh," she ended, slowly sliding her hands up around his neck.

"Why didn't you tell me?"

"Why should I tell you? You've never asked for my life story. But I would like to call you Josh, just when the film crew isn't around, of course."

"Of course," he agreed, pressing his forehead against hers in relief. She wasn't going to push, wasn't going to demand he tell her anything he didn't want to tell her. "You're one remarkable lady, Amanda Elizabeth Tremaine," he whispered almost reverently.

Mandy closed her eyes tightly, holding back a sob. No, I'm not, she wanted to scream. I'm only being this way because then I won't have to return the favor and tell you all about *me*. Tell you all about my past—about my grandfather's destruction of Dave Benjamin, or the part I played in the whole sordid mess. Oh, Josh, why can't we just stay here in Atlantic City forever, and let time stand still? "You're not so bad yourself, fella," she murmured against his chest while she blinked back tears.

And then, in the middle of the Flight Deck, with hundreds of people passing by on either side, they shared a kiss that proved not all the ringing bells and flashing lights in Slot City came with a price tag attached.

Or did they?

Mandy and Josh were still residing blissfully in a wonderful fantasy land usually reserved for the love-struck newlyweds the world believed them to be.

They had spent the entire afternoon strolling arm in arm through the huge Tropicana casino, dallying in the shops located in the hotel, sipping cool drinks in the sidewalk-café atmosphere of the Garden Terrace, and then braving the August heat outside to stand on the boardwalk and lift their faces to the sun.

By the time they had enjoyed a leisurely meal—dining in the Il Verdi restaurant and at last feasting on the northern Italian food they both favored—they were ready to face the film crew again for the staged dance scene in their hotel living room.

Understanding Chuck's problem with trying to light a scene correctly in a regular dance setting, Josh still found himself feeling slightly out of place as the technician turned on the four black boxes of flashing colored lights he had rented that afternoon to simulate a nightclub setting.

He stood quietly in a corner of the large room out of everyone's way, watching all the hustle and bustle around him, while occasionally glancing toward the stairs. Mandy seemed to be taking forever to get dressed, he thought, checking the time yet again on the slim gold watch on his wrist.

I know she said she was going to soak in the bathtub forever, he told himself as he tugged at his shirt cuffs and fumed, but this is ridiculous. Just as he took the first step toward the spiral staircase, bent on hustling Mandy along, he spied one black-high-heel-clad foot tentatively descending the first step.

The second foot followed closely behind the first, as did the smoky-gray-clad calves that rose from her slim ankles like perfect stems on some exotic flowers. He could just catch a fleeting glimpse of each dimpled knee as the curving of the staircase took her away from him even as it was bringing her nearer, and then she was standing on the bottom step facing him, and he drew in his breath sharply, as if in actual physical pain.

The simple black dress she wore hid more than it revealed, but it also hinted so blatantly at what treasures lay beneath it that Josh could feel his muscles tightening in automatic response. Never again would he accuse her of dressing like a teenager—at least not any teenager he knew!

The low, straight-cut bodice, held in place by two of the tiniest rhinestone-covered straps known to man, tugged slightly across her high breasts with every breath she took—an incitement to riot is how he would have described that slight stretching, he thought wildly, if anyone had cared to ask him for his opinion.

But it was her face that drew and held him, framed as it was in a glowing halo of freshly shampooed soft copper-red curls. Her eyes sparkled like huge emerald jewels from between her long darkened eyelashes, and the full red pout of her mouth looked moist, enticing. Even her spattering of freckles, which no amount of makeup could hide completely, looked sexy rather than cute.

Ivory was the perfect word to describe her creamy complexion, and his hot gaze traveled slowly down her long slim throat, then lovingly skimmed her bare shoulders before retracing their journey back up to her solemn, almost apprehensive looking face. *"I vant to bite your neck,"* he quoted crazily under his breath, amazing even himself with the depth of his passion for this small, gentle woman.

I don't think I'm falling in love with her, he corrected himself with a vehemence that startled him, I *am* in love with her. I, Joshua Mark Phillips, am hopelessly, madly, and passionately in love with Amanda Elizabeth Tremaine.

So, his saner self told him, you're in love with the woman. Now just what do you plan to do about it, buster?

I'm going to tell her exactly who I am, he reasoned rapidly, and I'm going to tell her how I only dreamed up that cockamamy story about Herb so that I could be near her—just like in those old Doris Day movies we joked about.

And then, you miserable busybody conscience, I am going to throw her over my shoulder and carry her off to the nearest justice of the peace just as fast as I can. *That's* what I'm going to do, he decided, straightening his tie with a decisive gesture.

And what about your plans for this videotape? his conscience asked, stopping him in his tracks. Are you going to tell her how you planned to send it to old Alexander Tremaine to punish him with the certain knowledge that you, one of Dave Benjamin's friends, was bedding down with his only granddaughter?

Oh, yeah, he mentally amended hastily as he completed his short journey across the living room to hold out his hand to Mandy, aiding her in her descent down the last step and onto the rug. I'm also going to cross my fingers and lie like hell, hoping she'll never learn about those other plans.

You mean you're never going to tell her? His better self was pushing now, not yet willing to let him off the hook.

Maybe when we're old and gray and bouncing our carrot-topped great-grandchildren on our laps, Josh temporized, but definitely not until then. Now cut me a break, my wife's waiting to dance with me. So thinking, he switched off his conscience, his better self, his saner self—and possibly even the major part of his rational intelligence—and gazed soulfully into Mandy's eyes as he lifted her hand to his lips.

"A treat well worth waiting for, madam. Darling, you look good enough to eat," he said for the benefit of none but Mandy and himself. "What do you say I toss these bozos out of here and the two of us get down to some serious necking?"

"*Joe*, for goodness' sake lower your voice," Mandy whispered in embarrassment, quickly looking around to make sure none of the television crew had heard him. Then she descended the last step and stood on tiptoe to murmur conspiratorially into his ear: "But I think something of the sort just might be arranged—later."

Wearing a smile that must have closely resembled that of Little Jack Horner as he pulled a juicy plum out of his Christmas pie, Josh stuck his hands deep in his trouser pockets and followed Mandy over to the coffee table and the tray of canapés he had ordered earlier.

As he walked, he whistled the melody of that great love song, "Tonight," from *West Side Story*.

Chapter Eight

The living room was in carefully orchestrated semi-darkness, with the four black boxes strategically placed so that their whirling, blinking lights, programmed to reflect the beat of the music, redefined the room into a thoroughly romantic setting.

Josh and Mandy stood close together in the center of the mock dance floor, Mandy having slipped out of her high heels so that she could move more easily over the carpeted floor. Her head, tucked comfortably beneath his chin, rested against the front of Josh's crisp white shirt. She could smell his spicy after-shave, feel the strong, even beating of his heart.

Josh had been holding her in a loose embrace, enjoying the faint tickle of her burnished curls as he lowered his head slightly to bury his face in their silky warmth. Slowly he disengaged his left arm from the embrace and took Mandy's hand in his own, raising it reverently to his lips just as Chuck signaled to Lois that the song she wanted was about to begin.

"It's perfect, absolutely perfect," Lois gushed quietly to Herb, who merely grunted, not wanting to take his attention from his camera. "I think we can get this in one take."

"To live with you forever my love..." came the low, throbbing words of the romantic duet Lois had selected as the perfect song for the filming started to fill the room. Josh smoothly adjusted his steps to the beat of the music, leading Mandy into a slow, sensual dance around the small area that was their own private dance floor, their own personal corner of heaven, their own soft cocoon filled with the warmth of their shared love.

The rest of the room faded away as they gave themselves up to the provocative music. "Give to me the treasure that is you..." the voices pleaded, rising into a crescendo of sound before Josh whirled Mandy around and around as a slow, throbbing drumbeat took them higher, ever higher.

"The wonder, the glory, the loveliness of love!" The song had been written for them, Mandy thought dreamily, created just for the two lovers slowly spinning and whirling within the circle of pulsating lights. Their arms woven tightly around each other, they moved to the left, held themselves suspended for a moment, then swayed gracefully, soulfully, before the beat of the music took them into another slow circular spin.

Josh lifted Mandy's right hand so that it met her other hand in a light clasp around his neck, then encircled her waist with his arms. Lifting her head and tilting back slightly in his embrace, Mandy stared up into his deep blue eyes. Her breath caught painfully in her throat as she saw the raw emotion shining from their depths.

The song was building to its blatantly emotional finale now and, as the lights cut the darkness with their enticing fingers of brilliant color, the dancers stood in the very center of the small dance floor, gazing deeply into one another's eyes as they spun slowly around...and around...and around.

Mandy felt like her head was a heavy blossom, tilting on its fragile stem as it was caressed by a soft summer breeze. She could feel the pressure of Josh's body against her own from breast to knee and instinctively pressed closer. It was his warmth she sought, just like a budding flower opening to its full potential under the heat of the summer sun.

She was floating, her stockinged feet moving effortlessly above the carpet. She was dizzy, but not from the movements of the dance. Oh, no, it was a dizziness of the heart that held her in its thrall, and she was powerless to fight it, did not want to fight it any longer, and hang the consequences. Mandy was a woman in love, and the love shone shamelessly from her eyes as a small smile curved her moist red lips.

Josh was lost, totally and completely lost. His entire world consisted of the beautiful woman he held so tenderly in his arms: Mandy of the emerald green eyes and the innocent, trusting heart. They could have been alone in the universe or in the middle of busy Times Square, it really didn't matter. They would still be alone, protected by the splendid isolation of their love.

He wanted the music to end so that he could pull her hard against his chest and crush her mouth with his own; he wanted the music to last forever so this feeling deep inside him could go on forever, filling him with a rush of tenderness so great he truly believed he could weep from the utter joy of it.

"Song's over," Herb announced prosaically, lowering his camera. "You wanna film this one, too?" he asked as the melody of yet another love song came from the tape deck.

Chuck shook his head in disgust, switching off all of the equipment except for the tape deck and the synchronized lighting system. "Don't you know when you're not wanted, you idiot?" he whispered, already taking Lois's arm and pushing her toward the door. "Come on, it's their honeymoon. Leave them alone for a while, huh?"

"But—but," Lois protested, still hypnotized by the sight of the slowly twirling couple, lost in each other as they moved around and around in a small circle to the beat of the music.

"But nothing," Chuck gritted, gesturing to Herb to get a move on. "We're history. Now *move!*"

The door closed softly, not quite latching, and Mandy and Josh were alone. Alone with the music and the lights and their love.

Out of the corner of one eye, Josh saw the crew leaving, and he nodded slightly to acknowledge Chuck's hand signal as the technician held up two fingers in a victory sign.

Reaching up behind him, Josh then took Mandy's hand and held it, pressing their joined hands close between them as he drew her more firmly into his embrace. "Alone at last," he breathed into her ear as he spun them around one last time, then laid her back over his arm in a flamboyant, old-fashioned dip.

Her hair hanging down over his sleeve, her moist lips slightly parted in mingled excitement and surprise, she breathed softly, "And do you plan to have your wicked way with me then, sir?"

The slow, lopsided grin she had learned to love appeared then as Josh let go of her hand, slipped his arm under her knees and lifted her high against his chest. "Shut up, woman, and point me toward the stairs," he answered, nuzzling her neck.

Mandy's arms held him tightly as she buried her flaming cheeks against his shoulder. "I love you, Josh whatever-your-name-is," she whispered, wanting him to know that it was more than the passion of the moment that had her agreeing to his plan.

Josh stopped, his foot on the bottom step of the spiral staircase that would soon lead them upstairs to the wide bed. "It's Josh Phillips, Ms. Amanda Elizabeth soon-to-be Phillips. And I love you too—more than I thought it was possible to love anyone."

"If that's a proposal, Mr. Phillips, I accept," Mandy answered quietly, fascinated by the intriguing way Josh's dark hair curved around the back of his ear. She leaned forward to press a soft, tantalizing kiss on the spot, reveling in the short gasp of pleasure that her action had provoked.

Josh stood there a moment longer, giving Mandy every chance to change her mind, but at last his hunger to possess her—to lie beside her and take everything she had to give, offer everything he longed to give her—won out, and he moved to ascend the staircase.

"What in blue blazes is going on in here? Joshua! Damn it, Josh, where are you?"

Josh froze in his tracks, his foot still raised, ready to mount the second step. *Dad!* his brain screamed silently as he shook his head in denial. It couldn't be his father, it just couldn't be. Not now, for God's sake. Please, Lord, not now!

"Josh?" Mandy pulled her head back slightly to look into her beloved's eyes. "Josh, let go. You're hurting me."

Belatedly, Josh realized that his arms had tightened instinctively around Mandy, holding onto her as if his mere physical grasp on her body could prevent the showdown he knew was coming. He moved backward until he was once more standing on the rug. "Sorry, darling," he whispered, easing his arm away so that her feet slipped to the floor and she stood close beside him, feeling somehow bereft.

At last Matthew Phillips located the switch just inside the door of the suite, and the living room was flooded with light. He looked around the room, taking in the blinking colored lights and the romantic music coming from the tape deck before his gaze was caught and held by the disquieting sight of the redheaded young woman clinging fearfully to his son.

"Looks like I've interrupted something, doesn't it, son?" he taunted angrily, walking across the room to switch off the equipment, dashing the last of the romantic mood Lois had so painstakingly created. "I can only hope I got here in time."

Mandy shook her head as if to clear it, a small frisson of fear running down her spine. "Got here in time for what? Who is this man, Josh? Why did he call you 'son'? Josh, answer me, what's going on?"

"I'm Matthew Phillips, Ms. Tremaine," he offered, holding out his hand as he crossed the room, and Mandy automatically held out her own hand as they observed the amenities. "Joshua's father, I'm ashamed to say. Why don't you come over to the couch and sit down, hm? I think it's time we all had a little talk."

Mandy looked up at Josh apprehensively. "Josh?"

Josh's arm tightened around her waist, and his eyes closed in resignation. "We'd better do as he says, Mandy. You're not the only one with a flair for the dramatic. I think Dad here is about to take center stage. Right, Dad?" he asked, throwing his father a sharp look.

"Shut up, Josh," his father bit out. "Ms. Tremaine...Mandy?" he urged, holding out his arm and gesturing toward the couch on the other side of the room.

Mandy threaded her way between the light boxes and over the snaking coils of thick black wire to perch nervously on the edge of the couch. "Josh?" Her eyes begged him to come sit beside her, to tell her everything was going to be all right, but he just shook his head and walked over to stare sightlessly at the closed drapes, his hands shoved firmly inside his trouser pockets.

Matt also declined to sit, choosing instead to pace back and forth in front of the coffee table, his head bent as he seemed to be studying the floral design on the carpeting.

Josh looks just like him, Mandy thought numbly. Is this how Josh will look in thirty years? That thought led to another: will I be around to see him in thirty years? Now why would I be wondering about that? she asked herself, taking a deep, steadying breath.

"Go for it, Dad, you've got the floor," she heard Josh say in a strange, tight voice.

"Don't be impertinent, Joshua!" his father snapped absently, still intent on his progress up and down the carpet.

"Mr. Phillips," she cut in nervously, "you seem to be angry with Josh. Is it something about the investigation?"

"The investigation?" Matt asked, stopping his pacing to stare a hole in his son's hunched back.

"Yes," Mandy supplied in a rush. "I know he didn't get too far with it here in Atlantic City, but Josh really has been working hard."

"I'll bet he has," Matt slid in nastily.

Mandy ignored the interruption to continue: "Josh thinks Herb is only a small part of a larger plan, and as soon as we return to Allentown he'll be able to locate the higher-ups. Isn't that right, Josh?" she asked, turning to him, hoping he'd say something—anything—to make his father understand. There *was* an investigation, after all, wasn't there? There *had* to be one, in order for Josh's father's presence here in Atlantic City to make sense at all!

"*Investigation*, Josh?" his father repeated, at last dropping into a chair. "My, you have been a busy fellow haven't you, son?"

Mandy may have been slow in reacting to the older man's presence, but she wasn't entirely stupid. Her heart sank to her toes. "There isn't any investigation, Josh, is there?" she asked brokenly. "Herb's just a cameraman, isn't he?"

"Who's Herb?" Matt put in, then waved his hand to negate the question. "Never mind, I don't think I even want to know."

Josh gave up his position in front of the drapes to cross the room and sit down beside Mandy, taking her suddenly cold hands between his own. "I made it up, darling, the whole thing. You were going to refuse to go on the honeymoon and I had to do something to change your mind." He gave her hands a quick squeeze. "Can you forgive me, Amanda Elizabeth? I was a desperate man."

Mandy looked longingly into Josh's eyes, quietly rejoicing in the knowledge that Josh would have done anything—even make up that silly story about Herb—to keep her from backing out of the planned honeymoon. Forgive him? How could she not, considering he did it just to be near her? "You're an idiot, do you know that, Joshua Phillips?" she said, smiling indulgently. She laid her head against his shoulder. "Of course I forgive you."

"Mandy!" Josh breathed, already turning toward her, intent on kissing her smiling mouth.

"If I may interrupt here," Matt said, rising once more to his feet. "This is all quite lovely, I'm sure, but I'm not here about any bogus investigation. Josh? Don't you think it's about time you leveled with this poor girl?"

"Not now, Dad," Josh gritted harshly. "Can't you see we want to be alone? There's plenty of time for explanations later."

"Explanations about what?" Mandy asked, agreeing that there had to be some very important information she was still lacking, considering the fact that Josh's father had traveled all the way to Atlantic City to talk to him. "What else don't I know?"

"Will you kindly move your miserable, lying self out of my way, please?"

Josh moved back half a step, allowing Mandy to get past him on her way into the bathroom. "For crying out loud, Mandy, stop this," he pleaded, going over to the bed and the open suitcase that lay there, closing the case with a determined snap. "Don't you realize we can't settle anything this way?"

Mandy emerged from the bathroom, her hands full of toiletries and two complimentary bars of soap. She dropped half of the unwieldy collection on the bed in order to flip open the suitcase, and disposed of the rest of the bottles of shampoo and bubble bath inside. "We can't settle anything, period," she told him coldly, turning back to the bathroom for another load.

As soon as she turned her back Josh flipped the open suitcase upside down, scattering the bottles and tubes of lipstick all over the bedspread before letting the case drop onto the floor. "I was going to tell you all about it, I swear I was, darling."

Mandy stuck her head out of the bathroom. "Oh, really? And when was that to be, Josh? Before or after you took me to bed?"

Josh grimaced as her thrust hit home.

Stomping back into the bedroom, Mandy picked up the suitcase and began replacing the toiletries Josh had dumped. "Tell me, Mr. Phillips of Southampton, Allentown and all points east, did you have Herb set up a secret camera in here, just so you could be sure to catch *all* the action?" She looked around the room, hunting for a hidden camera hanging from the ceiling.

"You know damn well I wouldn't do that!"

"How should I? You could have latent exhibitionist tendencies, for all I know. After all, I really don't know anything about you, Josh, do I?" She went over to the dresser and opened the top drawer, filling her hands with delicate undergarments.

"That's not true and you know it!" he protested, feeling he was beginning to lose touch with reality.

"Then please allow me to amend that last remark," she bit out, slamming the clothing into the suitcase. "I do know something about you—plenty, in fact. You're a low, conniving, lying—"

Josh grabbed up the undergarments, flinging them across the room with all his might, so that a silk ivory slip caught on a wall light to seemingly hang suspended in midair.

Mandy straightened, delivering Josh a long, dispassionate look, then walked across the bedroom with deliberate steps to retrieve the slip. Josh stepped in front of the bed, to keep her from replacing the slip in the suitcase. "Move it or lose it, buster," Mandy growled, her eyes shooting emerald fire.

Josh stepped to one side, knowing Mandy could try all night long to pack that suitcase, because he was going to keep on emptying it as fast as she could fill it up.

"Mandy—darling—listen to reason," he begged as she crouched on the floor, picking up the clothing he had thrown and flipping a succession of lace panties, pastel-colored bras and tangled panty hose in the general direction of the bed.

"'I'll not listen to reason,'" she quoted as she continued to toss undergarments until she had thrown them all onto the bed. "'Reason always means what some one else has got to say.' Elizabeth Cleghorn Gaskell." She stood up, brushing her hands against each other. "I did have a fairly broad classical education in Switzerland, you know, thanks to my grandfather's flair for finance."

"I only wish I had known you when you lived in Southampton," Josh said wistfully, marveling as yet another facet of Mandy was revealed to him. "Then we could have met like two normal people and avoided all this." He spread his hands to encompass the disordered hotel room as well as everything else that had happened since they met.

Mandy pressed a white-knuckled fist to her mouth and rocked back and forth slightly on her heels, her eyes closed tightly in pain. "No," she denied, turning away. "You wouldn't have wanted that, Josh, believe me, you wouldn't. I only wish we'd never met at all—ever."

"You still don't believe me, do you?" he cried, taking an impulsive step in her direction before common sense told him not to touch her for fear she'd shatter into a million small pieces at his feet. He swung away from her to slam a fist against the wall. "I could kill my father for telling you the way he did, not to mention the way he came barging in here once he thought he had put all the puzzle pieces together—like Sir Galahad riding to the rescue. If he had just phoned and confronted me with what he thought, I could have told him that I never would have used that tape. It was a stupid idea in the first place—I wasn't thinking clearly. I'd never consciously hurt you, Mandy, please believe that."

She pulled the second dresser drawer out entirely and walked to the bed, dumping the drawer's contents into the suitcase, then dropped the drawer an inch from Josh's foot. "Believe that?" she snorted, shaking her head. "Why not? Good old naive, trusting *dumb* Mandy. Just ask her—she'll believe *anything!*" She turned then, taking dead aim for the closet.

Josh scooped the pile of shorts and bathing suits out of the suitcase and stashed them under the pillow at the head of the bed. "At least tell me where you're going, for God's sake," he pleaded, ducking out of the way as a denim skirt, still attached to its hanger, flew through the air to land in the suitcase.

"As far away from you as I can get!" she answered from deep inside the closet. Two blouses exploded into the room, followed by a pair of white duck slacks and a sky-blue cardigan.

"Not in that dress, you're not!" Josh challenged fiercely, suddenly realizing that he didn't want Mandy out alone in that mind-blowing black dress.

Mandy emerged from the closet, looking hurriedly around the untidy room until she spied what she wanted. Snatching up the white slacks and the navy blue Penn State sweatshirt she had brought along in case it got cold on the boardwalk at night, she returned to the closet, closing the door behind her. The door then opened a crack as she ordered, "You stay right where you are. Don't even breathe." Then she pulled the door shut once more.

While Mandy was in the closet, Josh dumped the suitcase yet again, stuffing its contents under the bed, then added the suitcase, just for good measure. She wasn't going anywhere until he could talk to her, make her see that their love for each other was more important than his impulsive plan for revenge.

She had to listen to him. Ever since his father had explained how he had finally made the connection between the extra first prize in the contest and the telephone number of the Tropicana, Mandy had not been thinking, she had been reacting. Not that Josh could blame her, for he couldn't, not if he was honest with himself.

Almost bodily removing his father from the suite, Josh had run up the spiral staircase two steps at a time after Mandy, who had given a small cry and raced up the stairs as the full import of Matt's words had finally hit home. By the time he had caught his breath at the top of the staircase, she had already begun packing her suitcase.

It had been mayhem in the bedroom ever since.

The closet door opened sharply, banging against the wall beside it as Mandy, now clad in sweatshirt and slacks, her red hair a tangled mass of curls, marched around the room, searching for her sandals. Glaring at him for one long moment, she dropped to her knees to search under the wide bed, throwing out clothing and shampoo bottles until she had at last rescued her shoes.

She sat on the bed long enough to slip them on then returned to the closet to pick up the black dress and throw it straight into Josh's face. Then, giving him one last scathing look, she took up her purse and rapidly descended the stairs to the living room, leaving Josh where he stood.

"Hello, room service? This is Mrs. Tremaine in room—oh, you know the number? Good. I'd like to have Rollie Estrada sent to my room immediately, please," Mandy was saying into the phone as Josh came within earshot.

There was a moment of quiet before she spoke again. "Very well then, I understand. I desire a bottle of your finest champagne—no, make that *two* bottles—well chilled, and enough of your best imported caviar for a party of—" She hesitated a moment, deciding just how much she wanted Josh to pay. "A party of six, please." What the heck, she thought nastily; Josh could invite the television crew to the suite and they could all have a ball. *"Tout de suite!"* she then commanded regally. "Just make sure Rollie Estrada brings it, do you understand?"

A small smile curved her lips as Josh heard a strangled apology coming from the phone Mandy held away from her ear. "Yes, I thought you'd understand. Thank you *so* much," she replied coldly before slamming the phone back down on its receiver.

"Mandy—" Josh began, only to be interrupted by a loud knocking at the door. "Damn it!" he swore, throwing his hands in the air. "Nobody can move that fast!"

"Open this door, Joshua!" came the muted shout from the hallway. Josh spread his hands wide, palms up, as if to say, "Why the hell not?" and went to throw the door wide open.

"I don't know what I could have been thinking of, leaving the two of you alone," Matt Phillips was saying as he stormed into the room looking slightly disheveled. "Joshua, you haven't hurt this child in any way, have you?"

"No, Dad, I just tied her up and shoved bamboo slivers under her fingernails—nothing really sinister." Josh angrily ran a hand through his hair and flung himself down into a chair. "What are you back for, anyway? Haven't you done enough already? Or have you just stopped by to identify the remains?"

"Stop feeling sorry for yourself," Matt commanded sternly, looking at Mandy and realizing the slender hold the young woman had on her emotions. "Mandy?" he asked softly, taking a tentative step in her direction. "Is there anything I can do for you? Any place I can take you?"

Mandy looked at each of the Phillips men in turn, her narrowed eyes two chips of emerald ice. "I wouldn't cross the street with either of you!" she spat, going to answer the jaunty rapping at the door to allow Rollie, pushing a trolley holding two silver ice buckets and a huge domed serving platter, into the room.

"Evening, Mandy, Joe," the waiter said jovially, his nod of greeting also taking in the other occupant of the living room. "There's six champagne glasses on the tray—you guys planning on having a party or something? Don't tell me you wrapped up the filming already? Hey, where's the skinny blonde? What's her name? Lena? Lori? I wanted to talk to her."

Matt looked at Josh, hardly believing his son was somehow on a first-name basis with one of the Tropicana's waiters. "Who's Lena?" he whispered out of the corner of his mouth.

"Forget it, Dad," Josh said, rising to go over and put a detaining hand on Mandy's arm as she hoisted her purse to her shoulder, clearly intent on leaving. "Mandy, you can't just walk out on me like this," he implored, keeping his voice low.

"Just watch me, buster," she shot back, shrugging off his hand. "Your celebration feast has arrived—ordered by the victim herself. Have a ball!"

Pulling her stiff, resisting body into his arms, Josh went on unheeding. "I gave up the idea of revenge almost as soon as I thought it up, Mandy, I swear it. I haven't been stringing you along. I love you. Deep down inside—under all that hurt you're feeling right now—you know I love you. Please don't leave, Mandy, please."

She stood completely still in his embrace, her eyes closed as she bit her lip to keep from crying out. She wanted to stay, wanted to let him hold her in his arms and make her believe he loved her. She wanted it with every fiber of her being. Slowly, she allowed her body to relax just the slightest bit.

"It was a crazy thing to do, I knew it from the start," Josh told her in a rush, feeling her reluctant release of tension. "I must have been out of my mind. It's just that your grandfather has been a thorn in my side ever since I first found out he was the reason for Dave Benjamin's breakdown. Then, when I met you, I thought—"

With a heartrending sob, Mandy tore herself out of Josh's arms and ran for the door. "Rollie!" she called to the waiter, who was just uncorking the first bottle of champagne. "Take me to the nearest bus station. *Please!*"

The waiter looked toward the older gentleman, who seemed to look an awful lot like Joe Tremaine, and then at Mandy's husband. "What's going on?" he asked in confusion. "Lover's spat?"

The door to the hall had already closed behind Mandy, and Josh knew she wasn't coming back, even if she had to find the bus station without Rollie's help. Reaching into his pocket, he drew out a small stack of bills and thrust them into the waiter's hand. "Stay with her until the bus leaves, Rollie, and then come back to me and tell me where she's going. Can you do that for me, friend?"

Rollie opened his mouth to make a newlywed joke, saw the naked pain in Josh's eyes and wisely closed his mouth again. "Sure thing, buddy," he told him solemnly. "She'll never be out of my sight for a minute, I promise."

Josh stood looking at the closed door for a full minute after Rollie trotted out, as if he were thinking very hard—or praying. Then he turned and walked blindly toward the staircase, clearly intent on leaving the room.

"You're really broken up about this, aren't you, son?" his father asked, pouring himself a glass of champagne. "I thought about it after you threw me out earlier, and I called your mother in Southampton. She said it sounded like you might really be in love with this girl. Was she right, Josh? Are you in love with Mandy Tremaine?"

Josh turned to look at his father with suspiciously bright eyes. "What do you think, Dad?" he asked softly. "What do you think?"

Matt walked over to his son and slipped a comforting arm around his shoulders. "I think it's going to be a long night. Here—Mandy must have ordered this for you," he said, offering Josh the glass of champagne. "And, son—for what it's worth—I'm sorry."

Tilting back his head and raising his eyes to stare at the ceiling, Josh willed his voice to be steady. "Yeah, Dad," he whispered hoarsely, remembering the room as it had been an hour before, the lights dimmed, and Mandy like liquid fire in his arms. "So am I."

It was dark in the back of the bus, so dark that few people noticed the young woman huddled in the window seat, her legs tucked under her as she sniffled quietly into her handkerchief.

The full load of casino-goers exchanged stories of their exploits in the various casinos up and down the boardwalk as the bus rumbled along the Atlantic City Expressway, either bragging of their winnings or complaining over their losses.

"Hey, little lady," said one of the happier gamblers, leaning across the aisle to get Mandy's attention. "Nothing can be that bad, can it? You saved enough for the bus ride home, didn't you? After all, how much could a little girl have lost in one trip, anyway?"

"Not much," Mandy whispered, too quietly for the man to hear her. "Only my heart."

Chapter Nine

"That skunk!" Jeanne Tisdale said as she picked up a small stuffed animal and threw it against the nearest wall. "God, how I'd like to get my hands on that louse!"

Mandy had just finished telling her friend about her abbreviated "honeymoon" in Atlantic City, and Josh Phillips' plans for the videotapes from the trip. Jeanne was reacting with all the outrage and anger a good friend could show. So why, Mandy thought sadly as she sat perched on top of one of the large drawing tables in the playroom, her legs crossed at the ankles as they hung nearly to the floor, did she feel like she should be protecting Josh from that anger?

"He did say he wasn't really going to go through with it, Jeanne," she said now, nervously swinging her legs back and forth like a small child called before the teacher for some wrongdoing. "He said it was a dumb idea, and he knew it almost from the beginning."

"Well, three cheers for Joshua Phillips," Jeanne sneered, going over to retrieve the abused toy and dust it off before replacing it on the shelf. "Maybe we should nominate him for the Nobel prize."

"He thought he had a good reason for doing what he did—or almost did," Mandy pursued, slipping from the table to walk over to the large green blackboard. Picking up an eraser she found lying in the tray at the bottom of the board, she began rubbing off the chalk scribbles one of the children had drawn during the morning session. "I guess I can't really blame him all that much."

Jeanne whirled around swiftly and held out a hand in denial. "Oh, no, you don't, Mandy Tremaine," she protested, knowing what was coming. "You're not going to come crying to me, tell me about the rotten trick that guy tried on you and get me all hot and bothered—just so you can pull an about-face and *defend* the creep!"

"But—"

"But nothing!" Jeanne continued, running a hand through her hair and knocking her topknot to one side. "Next thing I know you'll be telling me the whole thing was *your* fault, and I won't have it, do you understand? You're a sweet, loving person, Mandy, but sometimes you're so damn *nice* it scares me."

"No, Jeanne," Mandy said, shaking her head ruefully in denial, "no, I'm not. You only think I am. Appearances can be deceiving—take it from me. To be quite frank, you really don't know anything about me, do you?"

Jeanne, highly insulted, pulled herself up stiffly. "You came to me three years ago with excellent references from that school in Switzerland. Nobody can play a role for three whole years, child. You're one of the good ones, and nobody could ever convince me of anything different. You're great with children—never playing favorites. You never complain about the low pay, and you're always ready to lend a hand in a crisis. What else do I have to know, for pity's sake?''

"You could have wondered where I come from, how I had lived before moving to Allentown, who my parents were," Mandy suggested, sticking a finger in the chalk dust that lay in the tray, then drawing a small stick figure on the blackboard.

Jeanne furrowed her brow in concentration, watching Mandy's hunched figure, which seemed to be burdened with some unseen weight. "That guy really did a number on you, didn't he? But you said he was after your grandfather—planning to use the videotape to avenge himself for something that happened a couple of years ago. You weren't directly involved, Mandy. You were only the innocent victim caught in the middle. Don't try to carry your grandfather's guilt around with you. Your grandfather's the one with the problem—him and that Phillips person."

Mandy looked down at her fingers, as if wondering how they had become covered with chalk, then started rubbing them with her other hand. "Out, out, damned spot," she mumbled brokenly, feeling the tears that were prickling behind her eyes. Funny, she hadn't thought there were any tears left.

Jeanne walked up to stand close beside her friend, her heart filled with sympathy for the young teacher's despair. "Mandy? Is there something you aren't telling me? Come on, sweetheart, nothing's so bad that it can't be fixed. Tell me about it."

Pressing her fist to her mouth as a shudder racked her body, Mandy turned to her friend, who opened her arms and gathered her into a motherly embrace. "There,

there," she soothed, rocking Mandy back and forth as she would an unhappy toddler, "you just have yourself a good cry. There's plenty of time for talk later, right?"

Mandy sat alone in a corner of the small enclosed playground, watching her class of happy three-year-olds as they played on the nearby swing sets. Two days had passed since her return to the nursery school, five days in all since her frantic flight from Atlantic City, and still she waited.

She waited each time the phone rang in the school office, expecting to be called to the phone.

She waited each day as she examined every envelope that came in her mail, wondering if he could have written her a letter of apology.

She waited for the sound of his shoes against the stairs, hoping against hope that he would come to see her, either to ask for her forgiveness or to demand that she admit her love for him—she really didn't care why, as long as he came.

But the only phone call she had been summoned to answer was one from Lois, who had told her she had packed up all Mandy's clothes at Josh's request and was sending the suitcase over by messenger.

Her only mail had come from Rollie, who had sent her a comic postcard displaying a message of thanks for allowing him to be included in the filming and the hope that she and her "husband" would be able to work things out.

And the only sound that broke the silence of her apartment on the long, lonely nights was the sound of her own weeping, as the realization slowly dawned that Josh was never going to arrive.

She had tried filling a few of those long evening hours by looking through the small pile of daily newspapers that had accumulated in her absence, only to open the financial section in one of them to see a grainy picture of Matthew Phillips staring out at her. "Phillips, Inc. Opts For The Media" the headline read, with the copy beneath the picture detailing the company's purchase of WFML's radio and television stations and giving both Matt's and Josh's names as the chief stockholders.

The story must have been released sometime after they had left for Atlantic City, she realized, understanding at last why Josh had not wanted her to know his real name. He must have been worried that the story would be published before they left and she might have made the connection even if his picture hadn't been shown.

She had cut out the story and read it carefully, learning that Phillips, Inc. maintained holdings in Basking Ridge as well as just outside Southampton, Long Island and many other towns in New Jersey, New York and Pennsylvania. WFML was just one of their many companies, and Josh had been working alongside his father ever since his graduation from Yale.

Dave Benjamin had gone to Yale, although he had dropped out in his junior year. Maybe that's when he and Josh first met, she had thought as she read the story. It didn't seem strange to her that Dave had never mentioned that one of his old college friends had moved to Southampton during her absence in Switzerland. After all, they hadn't really dated long enough to have gotten around to discussing every facet of each other's lives.

Long into the night, Mandy played out scenarios in her head, little scenes having to do with her chance meeting with Josh while out walking on the beach near her grandfather's estate; scenes that had the two of them instantly falling in love and then living happily ever after—with all of the heartbreak and misery of the past three years being replaced by three glorious years spent as man and wife. And perhaps, just to add to their joy, even a child.

But in the clear light of day those dreams vanished, leaving behind only the bitter truth that Josh had already had plenty of time during which he could have come after her—beating down her door if necessary—in order to prove that he had really meant it when he had said he loved her.

Not that his love would have survived the confession she would then be forced to make, the admission that his friend—the friend he had cared about enough to concoct his scheme for revenge—had nearly died because of her.

Mandy shook her head, bringing herself back to reality. Looking over toward the swings, she saw chubby little Missy Sanders rubbing one cornflower-blue eye while pointing an accusing finger at Christopher Rawlins, who was sitting on one swing while clutching a second one close to him by its chain. "Christopher, shame on you," she said gravely, reluctantly rising to go over and settle the little squabble before Missy burst into tears.

"He's only teasing you because he likes you, Missy," she told the child quietly, patting her blond head. "Boys are like that."

"Well, I don't like him back," Missy responded quickly. "I twink he's a twerrible person. He pulls my ponytail."

"Do you really pull Missy's ponytail, Christopher? *And* keep her from getting on the swings?" she asked the boy, kneeling down in front of him and taking hold of the swing on each side. "My, oh, my, you must like Missy an awful lot to do that. Why, I wouldn't be surprised if the two of you end up getting married some day."

Christopher thrust out his full bottom lip. "I do not like her," he grumbled, letting go of the other swing. "I hate girls. Girls are yucky. Here, Missy, take your dumb old swing."

"Another earth-shattering problem solved," Jeanne said as she walked up to stand beside Mandy as they both stood safely to one side and watched as Missy and Christopher tried to outdo each other in making their swings go the highest. "Are you feeling better now? You look better."

"I'm surviving," Mandy told her, brushing back a strand of hair that had blown across her eyes. "Forgive me for blubbering all over you yesterday afternoon. I really thought I was over the worst of it, or I wouldn't have come back to school."

"You had every right to blubber all over me, as you call it," Jeanne soothed, patting Mandy's shoulder. "But I still wish I could have convinced you that you're looking at this whole thing all wrong. If only you and Josh would get together—talk things over—I'm sure you could work it out."

Mandy looked at her friend and smiled. "I thought you were the one who wanted Josh Phillips tarred and feathered and run out of town on a rail. Why the change of heart?"

Jeanne clapped her hands together twice, signaling that playground time was over and it was time for the children's snacks. "Because I think the guy really cares about you, that's why. He's called here twice this week, asking me to let him know if you'd returned to classes. When he called for the third time this afternoon, I told him you were back."

"He called you? Why didn't you tell me?" Mandy looked around the playground, searching beyond the fence as if she expected to see Josh standing there watching her. "I thought he had probably gone back to Southampton with his father by now."

Jeanne shook her head. "They're both still here, working at the television studio, I guess. Josh didn't do anything more than ask for you the first two times he called, not that I knew it was him, considering I still thought you were in Atlantic City. But when he phoned today I recognized his voice and asked his name.

"I wanted to give him a piece of my mind, let me tell you, but he told me he had wanted to give you some time to think things over before he contacted you again. He figured you'd wait until you were calmed down before you came back to school, and be less liable to kick him down the stairs if he showed up at your apartment. The man seems to think you have a bit of a temper, love. I wonder where he got that idea," she ended, tongue-in-cheek.

"I'd never kick him down the stairs, anyway," Mandy muttered, hanging her head as she realized she probably would not have greeted him with open arms if he had shown up in the first two days after her return home. "He knows better than that."

They were busy for the next few minutes, herding the still restless children back inside the school, but Jeanne took a quick moment to whisper in Mandy's ear before going to her own classroom. "I really think the guy loves you, Mandy. When he comes to see you, why don't you level with him? He'll understand."

Mandy looked at her friend and smiled sadly, knowing that Jeanne thought she knew the full story behind her flight from Southampton. But she didn't; nobody did, except Mandy and her grandfather. "Thanks, Jeanne, I'll remember that if Josh really does show up," she promised as she shepherded Missy Sanders ahead of her into the classroom. "He'll never understand," she whispered under her breath after Jeanne had walked away. "And he'll never, ever forgive me."

Mandy perched tensely in one corner of the couch, nervously drumming her fingers on the upholstered arm. She had rushed home from the nursery school to bathe and wash her hair before eating a bowl of sugar-coated cereal for dinner, knowing she was too upset to do justice to a real meal.

She had changed her clothes three times, finally settling for her usual after-school outfit of cut-off denims and T-shirt, not wanting Josh to think she was expecting him to visit her tonight. Besides, she really wasn't expecting anything—she was praying for it!

The evening news had been over hours earlier, and she was pretending an interest in a summer rerun of some situation comedy she hadn't cared to watch the first time around. Maybe she should turn off the television and put on the radio—as long as she kept the living room filled with sound, so that she'd stop jumping at every little noise like some hysterical fool.

The phone rang on the television show and Mandy hopped to her feet, thinking it was hers. "That tears it!" she announced to the room at large, going over to snap off the set. "Much more of this and they'll be putting me in one of those lovely little places where everybody smiles a lot and weaves handmade baskets."

Then she fairly ran over to the radio, turning the volume up high to drown out the sudden silence that had enveloped the room once the noise from the television was gone. One of the boxes of saltwater taffy that she had found tucked into her suitcase was sitting beside the radio on the table. She eyed it owlishly for a few moments before deciding that even broken hearts needed sustenance once in a while, then ripped off the clear plastic seal.

Inside the box was a rainbow of colorful two-inch-long tubes of taffy decorated in different stripes for each flavor. Walking back over to the couch, she rummaged through the box, holding pieces up to her nose to sniff out her favorites. "Peppermint," she decided, eyeing a green-striped piece. "I'll eat this one first. After all, everyone knows its good form to have an after-dinner mint."

If one piece of taffy was good for the heart, then a second ought to be good for the soul, she reasoned, eagerly reaching for one of the few black pieces, which she was sure were licorice flavored. Her third selection was a truly delicious peach taffy, closely followed by a chewy piece of vanilla and then, just to show she was impartial, a piece of chocolate. "If I can find a strawberry taffy," she told herself as she dug to the bottom of the box, "I'll have hit the top three flavors."

Mandy was feeling just the tiniest bit queasy as she slipped a second piece of peppermint taffy into her mouth, but by now eating the taffy had become a challenge to her. If she ate a lemon taffy Josh would knock on her door before nine o'clock. If she followed the lemon with an orange-flavored one, he'd definitely be no later than the ten o'clock news. Ah, but if she ate this pretty pink one, he'd be here before she could even finish chewing it!

Unwrapping the pink taffy, she popped it in her mouth, bit into it to savor the flavor—and her chin immediately began to wobble. *"Watermelon!"* she wailed, suddenly remembering that last wonderful afternoon spent wandering through Slot City with Josh.

Slowly replacing the lid on the box, she gathered up the small mountain of empty taffy papers and shuffled barefoot toward the garbage can in the kitchen, still chewing on the memory-inducing watermelon-flavored candy. She stepped on the foot pedal that controlled the top of the can and dropped the wrappers inside, then let the lid drop with a bang.

That's funny, she thought, sniffling self-pityingly as she stared at the lid. I didn't think it made that thumping sound when it closed. She put out her foot and worked the pedal a few more times to compare the sound. It made a noise, but it wasn't a thumping sound. Was it possible to get drunk on saltwater taffy? She was hearing things. "I'll probably start hallucinating any minute now," she mused aloud, shaking her head as she began to make her way to the living room.

She had only taken a few steps when she heard the thumping sound again. Slapping a hand to her head she scolded herself: "It's the front door, you ding-a-ling! You're losing it, kid, you really are." Then, almost choking on the last little piece of taffy as she gave a loud gasp, she realized that Josh must have been knocking on her door and might already be thinking she wasn't home. She yelled, "Jus—just a minute! I'll be right there!" before skidding around the corner in her haste to catch him before he left.

She flung open the door and then leaned heavily against its edge, one hand to her breast and breathing hard, as if she had just run a record-setting mile. "Josh," she breathed, closing her eyes in mingled apprehension and relief. "I'm sorry I took so long to answer. You see, I didn't hear you until you knocked the second time."

She looked good enough to eat, and Josh had to forcibly hold himself back from taking her in his arms then and there. To cover his feelings he took refuge in a teasing response. "How would you know that my second knock wasn't my first knock if you didn't hear my first knock first?"

Mandy blinked twice, then shook her head. "You're beginning to sound more like me than me," she warned him, motioning with a wave of her hand that he should come in and sit down. "And, to answer your question, I did hear your first knock, only I didn't know I did. I thought you were the garbage-can lid."

Seating himself on the couch, Josh looked up at her, a sad smile on his face. "Why do I get the feeling Sigmund Freud would have a field day with that comparison?"

Mandy looked down at the floor, nervously kicking the fringed end of her small imitation Oriental carpet with one bare foot. "It—it's good to see you again, Josh," she said softly. "Lois sent back my suitcase."

"I tried to pack it myself, but I couldn't fold those silky things with my big hands," he told her, as if that explained everything. "It wasn't like I could keep anything from them anyway; not with Rollie damn near taking my head off for making you run away. They all like you a lot, Mandy. Herb said to tell you that you looked great on tape."

Mentioning the videotape was a truly brilliant move, Phillips, Josh told himself angrily as he watched the deep pink flush creep up Mandy's neck and into her cheeks. Why don't you tell her now that your dad said she seemed to be a "feisty enough female to tame you, son" and get your bigmouthed butt kicked out the front door before you can even begin to apologize for lying to her about your motives for going on the honeymoon in the first place?

"Did you—did you tell Herb that you were using him, playing him up to be some sort of criminal?" she asked now, finally deciding she had better sit down before she fell down.

"Dad took care of the explanations," he said, turning slightly so that he could look at her once she was seated in the chair beside the couch. "I don't know exactly what he said, but all three of them know their jobs depend on their convenient bouts of amnesia about the entire trip." He then took a deep breath before saying, "Look, Mandy, I didn't come here to talk about the film crew. I came to apolo—"

"To apologize, yes, I know," Mandy cut in hurriedly. "There's really no need for you to apologize, Josh. I understand why you did what you did. I'm just sorry that you did it all for nothing. Grandfather couldn't care less what I do, or who I do it with. You see, he disowned me more than three years ago."

Josh's mouth dropped open in surprise. "Disowned you? What the hell are you talking about, Mandy? He couldn't have disowned you. You disappeared without a trace. Tremaine made a big thing about it at the time, said he had private detectives out looking for you."

Mandy gave a wry laugh. "He's known all along where I am, Josh. That's why I didn't bother changing my name. That, and the fact that my teaching degree and letters of recommendation are all in my correct name. The only people I was hiding from were the press, and that was really only in the beginning. I've grown used to trying to stay out of the limelight, but I really doubt anybody cares about Amanda Tremaine of the South-ampton Tremaines anymore. Even you, Josh, were only interested in me because you thought I could help you hurt Grandfather."

Josh ran a hand through his hair, trying hard to understand. "I don't get it. Alexander Tremaine disowned his only grandchild? Why? It doesn't make any sense."

This is it, Mandy, she told herself. This is where you watch Josh's love for you turn into ashes. She had known ever since she had calmed down enough to give the matter some serious thought that sooner or later she would have to tell Josh the truth. "Grandfather disowned me because I accused him of trying to kill Dave Benjamin, even if I knew it wasn't entirely true." She took a deep breath and said the rest in a rush of words. "You see, Josh, *I* destroyed Dave, just as surely as if I was the one who ruined his company."

Mandy jumped up and went over to stare out of the window overlooking the street, unable to look at Josh now that she had said what had needed to be said, and it was quiet in the room for several minutes. Then, just as she thought she wouldn't be able to hold back her tears another moment, she felt his hand lightly touch her shoulder.

"Mandy...darling," he began hesitantly, "Dave Benjamin tried to commit suicide when his business went sour. Your grandfather bought up all his debts and was about to foreclose, so Dave decided to take what he thought was the easy way out. I liked Dave, but I don't consider what he did to be the act of a strong personality. You didn't have anything to do with his decision to try to end his life, you couldn't have—surely you can see that."

She whirled around to face him, leaving his hand suspended in midair. "Oh, no? Why do you think Grandfather set out to ruin Dave Benjamin? My grandfather may not be the nicest man in the world, but he doesn't just run around destroying people at random as some sort of twisted hobby. He purposely set out to ruin Dave because he didn't think Dave was good enough for his precious granddaughter. Dave told me all about it." She laughed almost hysterically before ending with a sob, "And I didn't even love Dave. I never intended to marry him. It was all for nothing."

She shook her head, her eyes shut tight against the condemnation she was sure she would see in Josh's face. "I couldn't face it, so I ran away with my tail between my legs. Grandfather's last words to me were to warn me not to come back until I grew up. *Oh, God!*"

Josh drew her unresisting body into his arms, cradling her against his chest as she broke into loud sobs. He didn't understand this, didn't understand it at all. Dave had never mentioned Mandy to him when they had occasionally met for lunch before his college friend had suffered his breakdown. Dave had only ranted and raved and cursed the greedy, power-mad Alexander Tremaine for deliberately running his company into bankruptcy.

Surely Mandy was blaming herself for something that wasn't her fault. And had been blaming herself for more than three years, he reminded himself with a grimace. Then, just as she was getting her life back together, I come on the scene and drag it all up again in the worst possible way. No wonder she ran from me the way she did. I'm just surprised she didn't punch me square in the nose!

Still holding her tight against him, he walked toward the couch and gently helped her to sit down. "Mandy," he urged, trying hard to lift her head from his chest, "you didn't destroy Dave; you didn't destroy anybody. Hey, didn't you tell me you couldn't even step on a spider? It was just a coincidence that you were dating Dave when your grandfather foreclosed. Dave was reaching, grabbing at any straw, telling you what he did. What did your grandfather say when you asked him about it?"

Mandy sat up and sniffed a time or two, searching in her shorts for a hankie. "I—I never did ask him," she admitted, blowing her nose. "I only saw him once after Dave's breakdown, and that was to tell him that I knew what he had done. He didn't deny it, Josh," she explained, looking up at him with tear-drenched eyes.

"So you ran away," Josh ended for her, using his own handkerchief to dab away her tears. "I imagine old Alex is still keeping tabs on you, waiting for you to come crawling back to him." He looked around the clean but inexpensively furnished room. "I'll bet it galls the hell out of him that you've managed to make it on your own."

"I'm not entirely helpless," Mandy told him, some of her former spirit coming back as she realized that Josh was still here, and not running away from her after her disclosure. "I ran away from Grandfather three years ago and I ran away from you five days ago. I guess I'm consistent, too. Right?"

Josh looked down at her, his slow lopsided grin making her heart do little flip-flops in her breast. "And here I was wondering how I could bring up the subject without having my head handed to me on a platter. You do know, Amanda Elizabeth, that the time has come to stop running?"

Her heart skipped a beat. "Meaning?" she asked, already knowing the answer.

"Meaning, my dearest love, that you and I are going to drive up to Southampton tomorrow to beard old Alexander Tremaine in his den. It's time you laid all your old ghosts to rest so that we can get on with our lives—together. Okay?"

Go back to Southampton? That was the last thing Mandy wanted to do. Josh didn't seem to agree with her theory that her involvement with Dave had nearly caused his death, but what if she was right? What if her grandfather agreed with her right in front of Josh? She couldn't bear it if Josh looked at her in disgust.

"Mandy? Hey, don't go getting all dramatic on me," Josh warned, pulling her close. "I can almost hear those wheels turning in your head. I love you, you darling creature, and nothing is going to change that. Understand?"

Slowly, Mandy nodded her head, her tears once more very close to the surface. "I love you, too, Josh. But what if I'm right, and Grandfather decides to take you on the way he did Dave? I don't think I could stand that. I love you too much."

Putting a finger under her chin to lift her head so that she was looking straight into his eyes, Josh said solemnly, "I'm a big boy, Mandy. I can handle your grandfather. Now, come here. We have some catching up to do. I believe we were in the middle of something rather important when my dear father interrupted us...."

Chapter Ten

Y ou're really going up there? What if Tremaine takes it into his head to throw you out on your ear? Hell's bells, son, from what I've seen of the old guy, I wouldn't be the least surprised if he sicced his dog on you.''

"Thanks for that rousing vote of confidence, Dad," Josh said dryly, stuffing some papers into his leather briefcase. "I'll be sure to stop along the way and pick up a couple of raw steaks just in case. But, please, once Mandy gets here I'd appreciate it if you'd keep your opinions to yourself. It took me most of last night to convince her to go up there in the first place."

"And the rest of the night?" The older man leaned back in the swivel chair behind his desk at the television station, a knowing smile on his face. "You never did say how you two passed the time until you showed up here this morning. Perhaps you whiled away the time with a few rubbers of honeymoon bridge?"

Josh gave his father a dirty look. "Mom really must have her hands full keeping you in line, you randy old goat. We *talked*, Dad. We filled each other in about our childhood and college days, things like that." He walked over to a file cabinet to get another paper he really didn't need. "Did you know that Mandy's parents died in a boating accident when she was only about three years old?"

"So the old man raised her?" Matt put in reflectively, tilting the chair back so that he could rest one foot on the desktop. "She must have had a charming childhood."

Josh stopped what he was doing to sit on the edge of the desk and stare into the distance at nothing in particular. "You know how the experts say people try to block out unpleasant memories? Well, Mandy swears she can't remember anything under the age of twelve, except for a few isolated incidents."

"And those memories?" Matt prompted, frowning. He hadn't seen much of Mandy Tremaine, but what he had seen he had liked—very much. It didn't sit well with him to think she might have been an unhappy child.

"Bad ones—all bad. Her parents' funeral, the day her favorite nanny left, the summer her teeth braces came off and her grandfather said she still looked like she came from the wrong side of the family."

Matt was quiet for a minute, his lips pressed together in a firm line. "Maybe I'll go with you, son," he said at last. "I think I'd like to get a few good licks in on this guy myself."

"Mandy may not admit it, but she still loves her grandfather," Josh told his father thoughtfully. "His opinion still seems to matter to her. I think she's spent her whole life trying to measure up to his expectations of her.

The private schools in Switzerland ever since she was fourteen, that sort of thing.''

''Then she comes home and immediately becomes involved with Dave Benjamin, a man her grandfather disapproves of?''

Josh stood up and walked over to the clothes tree in the corner to get his sport coat. ''He didn't disapprove at first. As a matter of fact, he fairly pushed her at Dave, but it didn't take. Mandy liked him, but she already knew the relationship wasn't going anywhere.''

''Yet she blames herself for his breakdown. What happened, did they have an argument?'' Matt was still trying to fit all the pieces into the puzzle that had led to Mandy's flight from Southampton.

Josh shook his head in answer to his father's last question. ''No, *they* didn't argue. She and Alexander argued. The old man said he had discovered Dave to be weak, and he didn't want her seeing him anymore. But Dave kept calling her, begging her to see him. That's when Dave told her that Tremaine was out to ruin him because of his interest in her. From that point on, things got pretty messy.''

Matt nodded his head, already perceiving the rest of the story. ''Mandy went off hotfoot to her grandfather to protest his poor treatment of Dave and the two of them had their first real battle of wills, right? That in itself must have been fairly traumatic for her. Then Dave tries to commit suicide and everything hits the fan, right?''

''You've got to admit Dave was pretty personal about the thing—shooting himself on the old man's front steps. Mandy heard the shot from her bedroom and was the first to find him lying there wounded. After that, all that remained was her last violent scene with her grandfather before she packed her bags and drove away from Southampton, to end up here in Allentown. Her car broke down about five miles out of town, and she figured it was an omen, or some such thing. She's been here ever since."

"Until she entered a radio contest and ended up on a bogus honeymoon with Dave Benjamin's old college buddy." Matt dropped his leg to the floor, pulled the swivel chair forward with a snap and laid his forearms on the desktop. "It just goes to prove that old adage—you may run, but you can't hide. Poor girl. Make sure you stay overnight with your mother. I already called and told her to expect you and a guest. I think Mandy could do with a good dose of your mother's tender loving care."

Josh's face brightened perceptively. "Mom's going to love her, Dad, and so will you. You didn't quite see her at her best the other night, which was my fault."

"It was your fault all right, son," Matt said, chuckling reminiscently. "But don't think I wasn't impressed with Mandy. She reminded me of your mother that time I—well, never mind about that."

Snapping his briefcase shut, Josh continued earnestly, "Mandy's just about the greatest thing that has ever happened to me. I figure we can be married from the house in Basking Ridge—not in Southampton—unless things turn out better today than I think they will." He cocked his head to one side, listening to something he heard just outside the door. "That's Mandy now, talking to the secretary. Don't let on I've told you anything, okay?"

"Well, that's stupid," Matt began testily. "I *was* in Atlantic City with you two, remember? She knows I know, you know I know—so how in blue blazes am I supposed to play dumb without looking dumb? Lord, Josh, falling in love seems to have rattled your brains. I—"

"Mandy! Come in, darling, and see who's here. Don't just stand there hanging onto the doorknob," Josh exclaimed loudly, cutting off his father's words as he crossed the room quickly to give her a warm welcoming kiss on the lips. "Dad? You remember Mandy, don't you?" Josh's eyes were full of warning when he looked at the older man.

"Of course I remember Mandy," Matt said jovially, rising to his feet to come around the desk, holding out his hand. "And I enjoyed the champagne and caviar very much, thank you, although I enjoyed the look on Josh's face even more when he saw the bill." He enclosed Mandy's hand in his own larger one and gave it a quick squeeze. "Come on over here and sit down. Josh was just telling me—"

Josh cleared his throat noisily, earning himself a derisive smile from his father.

"Josh was just telling me," he continued undaunted, "that the two of you are driving up to Southampton this morning, and I was making sure he had planned on spending the night at our house. My wife's anxious to meet you." Then, turning to his son, he ended, "There. Was that all right, teacher, or are you going to rap my knuckles?"

Mandy looked back and forth between the two men, feeling the affection between them, and smiled in understanding. "You'll have to forgive Josh, Mr. Phillips. He seems to think I'm more fragile than I am. I imagine he told you everything?"

Matt slipped a protective arm around Mandy's shoulders and led her to a chair. "I beat it out of him, actually," he said, choosing to spare his son if Mandy became angry, which she showed no signs of doing. "For what it's worth, I agree with my son. You have to go and have it out with your grandfather once and for all. It's the only way you'll ever feel at peace about the whole thing.''

"Not only do you two look alike, but you think alike as well. I only hope you're right," Mandy replied candidly. "And I don't mind that Josh told you why I disappeared from the scene the same week Dave had his breakdown. I called my grandfather once I was settled here in Allentown, but I guess by then he didn't feel it was necessary to tell anyone where I was. I think he believed I'd be back under his roof within a month.''

"I imagine your disappearance would have caused more of a stir if it hadn't happened so close to Dave's attempted suicide," Matt supplied thoughtfully.

"That, and the fact that I was rarely in Southampton once I reached my teens," Mandy added quietly. "I didn't really have any friends in the area who would care where I was.'' She looked down at the purse in her lap, realizing that she had been nervously snapping and unsnapping the clasp. "Sorry," she said, moving her hands so that she was holding onto the chair arms, "bad habit.''

Josh spoke to fill the awkward silence that fell after Mandy's last words. "Hey! Look at the time. Mandy, if we're going to get there before the rush-hour traffic we'd better get on our horses.'' He turned to his father and gave him a broad wink. "Dad, think you can handle things here while we're gone?''

"Think you're smart, don't you, son?" Matt shot back in mock anger. "Mandy, try to do something about this superiority complex of his, will you?" he asked, shaking his head, but not quite hiding his pride in his only son. "Lord knows his mother and I have tried, but—" He let his words fall off meaningfully.

Mandy stood up and went over to the older man, standing on tiptoe to kiss his lean cheek. "Don't worry,

Mr. Phillips," she confided softly. "I have a feeling he's going to grow up to be just like you. I wouldn't change a hair on his head."

Josh was standing at the office door, holding it wide, his sport jacket hooked over his shoulder on one finger. "Stay away from my woman, Dad. You've got one of your own, remember?" he growled cheerfully.

"Spoilsport." Matt grimaced, then returned Mandy's kiss, whispering in her ear. "And call me Matt, please." Then he waved the two of them on their way.

When they were gone, he went to the phone and rang for an outside line. He wanted to call his wife and tell her she was right—their son had finally found the right woman.

Mandy's slim body lay resting against the passenger door of the car, her head cradled against one curved hand as she slept. Josh had noticed her eyelids growing heavier as they turned onto the New Jersey Turnpike, and had purposely stopped talking. It hadn't been long before the easy-listening music coming from the car radio had soothed her into slumber.

She looked like a little girl with the seat belt strapped around her simple yellow sundress. But Mandy was no child, Josh acknowledged thankfully as he followed the path of the shoulder harness as it rested against the soft swell of her gently rising and falling breasts.

How would she handle it if Alexander Tremaine refused to see her, or, even worse, if he agreed with her belief that she was at the bottom of Dave's breakdown? She'd be devastated all over again, as she had been three years ago.

Josh's jaws worked as he resolved that this time it would be different. This time, no matter what the result of their meeting with Tremaine, Mandy wouldn't be left to go off somewhere all alone to lick her wounds. And you'll never be alone again, he promised silently, taking his hand from the wheel to run a finger softly down the side of her sleep-flushed cheek.

He had been driving almost automatically for some time now, and they were within a dozen miles of Southampton. Already he could smell the warm tangy aroma of the sea, as tall grasses and little spits of sand lined the roadway.

He'd better give her some time to collect her thoughts, he decided, reaching over to touch her bare arm. "Mandy, honey, time to wake up," he prodded, taking his attention from the road just long enough to see that she was staring wide-eyed out the side window, hardly believing she had slept so long.

"Oh, I'm so sorry," she apologized, running her fingers through her hair in an effort to bring some semblance of order to the riot of curls. "I hadn't realized I was so tired. We're almost there, aren't we?" she asked in a small, quavering voice.

Alexander Tremaine had built his estate on the near outskirts of Southampton and Josh was soon turning onto a smaller roadway that would eventually join with Tremaine's private drive. "I still think we should have phoned ahead," he said, looking at his watch and seeing that it was only four in the afternoon. "He may not be home."

Mandy giggled nervously. "Honestly, Josh, you sound like an ad for the phone company. Don't worry," she added, her tone suddenly serious, "Grandfather will be home. He's a creature of habit, and he hasn't stayed at his office past two-thirty in twenty years. Since my parents died, in fact. The turn's just ahead now, Josh, to the right.''

Although she had every right to be apprehensive about the coming meeting, Mandy seemed to be sitting up straighter as the car moved closer to their destination. Her voice seemed firmer, her chin tilted at a more determined angle.

Alexander Tremaine may have chased away a badly frightened, confused girl, but he was getting back a mature woman, capable of giving back as good as she got. Josh felt his chest swell with pride, believing his own advent into Mandy's life may have helped her feeling of self-assurance.

"There it is!" Mandy said with a gasp. "I had forgotten how really *big* it is." Alexander Tremaine really built himself quite a house, Josh thought admiringly as he pulled the car to a halt in front of the great oaken door of the Tudor mansion. It was only as he was extracting the key from the ignition that he realized that Mandy still hadn't unbuckled her seat belt. She was sitting rock still, staring at the concrete steps in front of the mansion.

"That—that's where I found Dave," she told him softly, before averting her eyes to stare straight ahead. "It was only a flesh wound, but there was so much blood! For a moment I thought I could still see him lying there. Silly, isn't it?"

Josh used the lever on his side of the car to unlock Mandy's door and went around to open it from the outside. Holding out his hand to her, he silently bid her to come with him.

"Miss Amanda," the middle-aged man Josh took for the butler said when he answered their knock, showing no surprise at her presence after such a long absence. "Mr. Tremaine is in his study, as you'll know."

"Yes, thank you, Farnsworth," she answered, reaching for Josh's hand as she began walking through the three-storied foyer toward the back of the house.

"Not exactly killing the fatted calf, is he?" Josh whispered into her ear as they followed the butler, who had hastened to precede them. Looking around at the dark paneled walls and darker oil portraits that lined them, he added, "Why do I keep thinking Vincent Price is going to show up at any minute and serve henbane tea?"

His jokes had the desired affect, and Mandy squeezed his hand tightly as she smiled up into his face. "Close your eyes a moment and imagine what happened the day I tried leaving my skateboard in this foyer. Obviously Farnsworth hasn't forgiven me yet."

Then they were at the end of the hall and the butler was holding the study door open for them so they could enter. Mandy went first, stopping only a few steps inside the door, Josh close behind her. When the butler seemed to linger, he turned and said sternly, "That will be all, Farnsworthy, thank you. You may go."

"That's Farnsworth, sir," the butler intoned icily.

Josh looked the man up and down, letting him know he had purposely used the wrong name. "Whatever," he answered offhandedly, feeling he had avenged Mandy a little when he saw the chagrin on the butler's face. Then Josh turned his attention to a quick inventory of the room, which was tightly draped against the sunlight.

It looked like the law library of some old established Philadelphia firm, he decided, his gaze traveling over the book-lined walls and inventorying the leather couch and matching wing chairs to finally focus on the huge mahogany desk that sat in front of one of the velvet-draped windows.

The man who sat behind the desk didn't look imposing, he thought. He just looked old, old and wrinkled and tired. He hadn't looked up at their entrance, seemingly absorbed by the papers he held in front of him. He looked, Josh decided, about as threatening as a basset hound.

"I told you I didn't want that damned medicine, Farnsworth," the old man growled without looking up, "so you can just take it back to wherever you got it from, understand?"

"It's not Farnsworth, Grandfather," Mandy explained, moving another tentative step into the room. "It's me, Mandy. I've come to talk to you, if you don't mind."

Alexander Tremaine looked up over his half-frame reading glasses, his failing sight piercing the dimness as he followed the sound of his granddaughter's voice. "Who's that with you?" he asked coldly. "What's the matter, child, afraid I'd bite your head off if you came alone?"

"My name is Joshua Phillips, sir," Josh explained emotionlessly, stepping past Mandy to walk over to the desk, his right hand extended. He held it out long enough to count slowly to ten, and then let it drop to his side.

"I know who you are, Phillips, *and* what you and my granddaughter have been up to," Tremaine informed them, leaning back in his oversize leather chair, apparently enjoying the fact that it creaked loudly with his every movement. "Amanda Elizabeth has never been out of my control, no matter how much she thinks she is. According to this report in front of me right now, it would appear she is just as naive and foolish as she was the day she left me—*here*." He looked Josh up and down appraisingly. "An investigator? You? You don't even wear crepe soles, for God's sake. Playing house with my granddaughter, were you? How much will it cost me this time?''

Mandy had taken enough, and she forgot her fears as she raced to Josh's side, just as he was about to open his mouth and say something she was sure he'd regret later. ''Josh and I are going to be married, Grandfather,'' she put in firmly. ''I won't allow you to talk to him that way, do you understand?''

''You *won't allow* it, will you, missy!'' Tremaine exploded, rising to his feet. ''Do you have any idea what it cost me the last time? Half a million dollars, that's what, and then the cowardly fool goes and pretends to blow his head off on my doorstep when it wasn't enough, so that I've been footing the bill at that fancy private hospital for three years while he chases the nurses. Not that I care about that, because I don't. But he really made me pay, didn't he, when you left me?''

Mandy stood there wide-eyed, slowly turning her head back and forth, as the truth finally hit her. ''You *paid* Dave Benjamin to stay away from me? But I thought you forced him into bankruptcy. Grandfather, I don't understand.''

Josh stood quietly beside Mandy, thinking hard. ''Dave was lying all along, wasn't he, Mr. Tremaine? He lied to you about the depth of his involvement with Mandy, and to Mandy about the reason for his money problems. And when the money you gave him still wasn't enough, he faked a public suicide so that he could be put in an institution away from his creditors. What was it— gambling?''

Alexander Tremaine looked at Josh with dawning respect. ''Very good. You've got it right in one, Phillips. Maybe you're not as dumb as you look, pretty boy. Although only a woman would believe a person could try to blow his brains out at point-blank range and end up with a flesh wound that didn't even need stitches! Dave Benjamin is about as crazy as a fox.''

"Yet you're paying for his hospitalization," Josh remarked, winking at the older man. "Why do I get the feeling you're not as bad as your press paints you?"

"My investigator says you're half of Phillips, Inc.,'' Tremaine said, changing the subject. "Tell me, do you hold up your own end, or are you just another daddy's boy?''

Josh smiled broadly, slipping his arm around Mandy's shoulders and pulling her close. "I can run rings around you any day, old man, if you push me. Does that answer your question?''

The older man threw back his head and laughed, a dry, papery sound, as if he hadn't found much in his life to amuse him. "Mandy, I think you can keep this one," he said approvingly.

But Mandy was still trying to understand exactly what had happened three years ago. It hadn't taken her any longer than it had Josh to figure out that Dave Benjamin had made victims of them all, but she still couldn't explain why her grandfather had let her leave, still believing what she had about their involvement with Dave's attempted suicide.

"Why did you let me leave?" she asked finally, putting her thoughts into words. "I know you never liked me much, but I didn't think you hated me. I was hurting when I left here, Grandfather. Hurting bad.''

"You were *sulking*, child, just like you always did, turning the whole sordid mess into trashy melodrama, with yourself cast in Joan Crawford's role." He turned to Josh, confiding good-naturedly, "She was always a dreamer, weaving fantasies in her head. I was the Black Prince, I believe, ever the villain. But she's got a good head on her shoulders. I knew she'd be back one of these days—when she grew up.''

Mandy walked around the desk to stand eye to eye with her grandfather, for he was not a very big man. ''Grandfather,'' she asked, her voice low with intensity, ''did you ever love me—even a little?''

Josh thought Alexander Tremaine looked more like a worn old basset hound than ever as he tentatively put out a hand and stroked Mandy's cheek. ''I love you enough to be willing to put up with a bunch of carrot-topped great-grandchildren, Amanda Elizabeth, if that answers your question. Hey, stop that,'' he warned happily, ''I'm too old and frail for such treatment. Amanda Elizabeth, stop hugging me at once, do you hear!''

''Your medicine, sir,'' came Farnsworth's superior tones from somewhere behind Josh.

Josh looked at the butler, standing stiff and straight, a small silver tray in his hand, and then over at Mandy and her grandfather, locked together in a healing embrace. He turned to Farnsworth, a rueful smile on his face. ''Mr. Tremaine has already got his medicine, Farnsworth. I don't believe he'll be needing you at the moment.''

Rollie Estrada softly closed the door to the Concierge suite at the plush Tropicana Hotel, his wide toothy grin very much in evidence as he pocketed the large tip Josh had just handed him. ''I do love a happy ending,'' he said to no one in particular before placing the Do Not Disturb sign on the doorknob and walking away, whistling under his breath.

* * * * *

Take 4 Silhouette Desire novels
and a surprise gift

Then preview 6 brand-new *Silhouette Desire* novels—delivered to your door as soon as they come off the presses! If you decide to keep them, you pay just $2.24 each*—a 10% saving off the retail price, *with no additional charges for postage and handling!*

Silhouette Desire novels are not for everyone. They are written especially for the woman who wants a more satisfying, more deeply involving reading experience. *Silhouette Desire* novels take you beyond the others.

Start with 4 Silhouette Desire novels and a surprise gift absolutely FREE. They're yours to keep without obligation. You can always return a shipment and cancel at any time.

Simply fill out and return the coupon today!

* Plus 69¢ postage and handling per shipment in Canada.

COMING NEXT MONTH

#544 THAT'S WHAT FRIENDS ARE FOR—Annette Broadrick
Brad Crawford had once loved Penny Blackwell so much he'd been
willing to let her go. But now Brad was back and determined to save
Penny from marrying the wrong man. After all, to love, cherish and
protect—isn't that what friends are for?

#545 KANE AND MABEL—Sharon De Vita
Kati Ryan's diner was her pride and joy, so sparks flew when Lucas
Kane showed up, claiming to be her new partner. Luke needed a
change of scenery and Kati fit the bill—he'd show her they were both
born to raise Kane.

#546 DEAR CORRIE—Joan Smith
When it came to Bryan Holmes, columnist Corrie James knew she
should take her own advice—"no commitment, no dice." But this
romantic playboy was simply too sexy to resist!

#547 DREAMS ARE FOREVER—Joyce Higgins
Cade Barrett was investigating Leigh Meyers's company for
investment purposes, but in her he found a more valuable asset. He
wanted her for his own, but she'd given up on childhood dreams of
happy endings. He'd have to prove that dreams are forever....

#548 MID-AIR—Lynnette Morland
Whenever Lorelei Chant worked with pilot-producer Chris Jansen,
his sky-blue eyes made her heart soar. The trouble was, Chris seemed
to like flying alone. Could Lorelei convince him that love can happen
in the strangest places—even in mid-air?

#549 TOUCHED BY MAGIC—Frances Lloyd
Architect Alexandra Vickery's new client, Lucien Duclos, was quite a
handful—arrestingly attractive and extremely suspicious of women
designers. Alex was determined to prove herself, but how could she
keep her composure when she discovered he was as attracted to her as
she was to him?

AVAILABLE THIS MONTH:

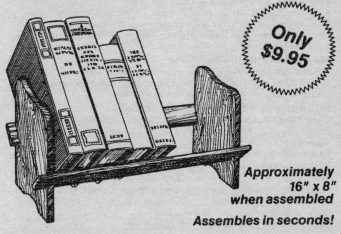